The Sewing Machine Man

'I don't think I'm going to let you go. I think I'm going to keep you here for ever, locked in the wardrobe during the day and in here . . .' she took my hand and placed it on her tummy, '. . . all night. How would you like to be a kept man, Russ, baby?'

I gave her a kiss that told her exactly how the idea appealed to me and, so help me, she started coming to the boil again.

Just ringing a few d........
world for Russ To.......
hot-blooded male.

By the same author in Mayflower Books

THE DEBT COLLECTOR
OCTOPUS HILL
THE COURIER
COME AGAIN COURIER
TOBIN TAKES OFF

To come

TOBIN ON SAFARI

The Sewing Machine Man

Stanley Morgan

Mayflower

Granada Publishing Limited
Published in 1969 by Mayflower Books Ltd
Frogmore, St Albans, Herts AL2 2NF

Reprinted 1969 (three times), 1970 (three times),
1971 (three times), 1972, 1973 (three times)

Originally published by the Harcourt Press
Copyright © Stanley Morgan 1968
Made and printed in Great Britain by
Richard Clay (The Chaucer Press), Ltd.,
Bungay, Suffolk
Set in Linotype Times

The Sewing Machine Man is a work of fiction.
Any similarity between its characters and real
persons, either living or dead, is not only
accidental and unintended but also quite likely.

The world is full of such beautiful girls,
The long, the short, and the tall,
But one thing I know
depresses me so,
I can never make love to them all,
No,
I shall never make love to them all.

A LUSTY'S LAMENT—Composed by
Russ Tobin on
the Liverpool–New Brighton Ferry

ONE

It was going to be another one of those days; I could tell that the moment I opened my eyes and saw daylight. There shouldn't have been any, you see, not at that time of the year. At seven o'clock on a January morning my little back room's as black as a coal heaver's armpit, and, some might be rude enough to remark, not too dissimilar in other respects. It does get a bit close in there, I'll grant them, but then there isn't much choice really. If I open the window I freeze to death and that's the only alternative that comes to mind immediately.

Anyway, I was late—again, that's what I'm driving at, and on a Friday, too, the busiest blinking day of the week down at Wainwright's. And there, standing on the bed-side table, grinning all over his stupid face and marching along in time with the ticks and the tocks, was the culprit—Mickey Mouse. About once every three months he had one of his funny turns and his bells didn't ring and then he'd put me right in it. Oh, it's my own fault, I know. I should have pensioned him off ages ago and got a new clock, and I'd thought about it too, dozens of times, but I didn't have the heart somehow. He'd been with me so long it would've been like eating a pet rabbit.

Just for spite, though, I reached out and clipped him one and blind me if he didn't start ringing—exactly one hour too late. Eight o'flamin' clock on a Friday morning.

I skipped out of bed and pulled the curtains. God, wouldn't you know it, it was raining again. Bucketing down. It was falling off the grey slate roof of the house at the back of ours like Victoria Falls, and at one place where the guttering was broken it was dropping in a solid pipe of water that looked stiff enough to punch holes in the back yard.

As I was watching it, feeling my spirits dropping with the rain, the kitchen door of the other house opened and old man Mathews came out all dolled up in his sou'wester and gaiters like a deep-sea fisherman. He ran to open the double doors into the alley which separates our row of houses from his and then he tried to start his motor bike. He'd had it covered with his wife's old plastic mac, but it hadn't done much good. He jumped up and down on the kick-start like he was stomping it

7

to death and then his foot slipped off and he cracked his ankle a beaut. Even from that distance I could hear the language, but I wasn't too sorry for him because he's a dirty old devil; he spits in the street and I can't stand that.

Well, there was no time to stand there watching old Mathews. I'd have to get a move on. I put on my dressing gown and picked up all my shaving stuff and went out on to the landing.

It's a pretty big house, Ravenscourt, and more big than pretty. It's in . . . well, look, let's do the thing properly and just explain what I'm doing there and then you'll know what I'm going on about.

For a start, I'm called Russ Tobin and I'm free, white and twenty-two. Well, white, I certainly am, and who wouldn't be in this God-forsaken climate; as for free, well, I'm as free as anybody ever is when they've got the mind-boggling sum of three quid a week to lavish on themselves after all the expenses are paid.

I was born in a suffocatingly cute village in Cheshire (which we shall call Nether Piddlington, just in case any of the seventy-five inhabitants of the real place happen to read this) which has five pubs (named, unbelievably, The Crown, The Red Lion, The Dog and Duck, The Rose and Crown and The Plough), a cute, old twelfth-century church which is run by a senile vicar named Glastonbury who delivers cute twelfth-century sermons to anybody who has nothing better to do than listen to him, which apart from Easter, Christmas and Remembrance Sunday, is usually just the choir, the bell ringers and the old sexton, who is as deaf as a yard of pump water anyway. And if you don't call that a captive audience, I'd like to know what is.

I must have been all of ten before I realized just how suffocating my environment really was and began yearning for something to happen. Oh, how I longed for the big cities of maybe five, or even six, hundred people; how I dreamed that one day I too might see a real talking movie picture instead of the 16-mm. silents that Baldy Yates showed us in the village hall every Saturday afternoon.

Fortunately, my father was a man of vision, a mental giant in a land of dart-slinging, ale-swilling, muck-spreading pigmies. He sent me to grammar school.

Unfortunately, however, I had been sufficiently rurally retarded by the age of eleven that I missed the genius boat by a hell of a long jump and I landed with an academically clumsy splash just this side of mediocrity. Not that I haven't got all my marbles—those I most certainly have. But instead of the gleaming, blood-red pollies my father had hoped for, they more closely resemble the green glass stoppers that used to bung up pop bottles in the old days.

But, what the heck. Cleverness, like everything else, is relative; it depends on the company you keep.

After school I was too big for the village. It had shrunk, term by term, during my years at school until, then, at the age of sixteen, it smothered my senses like a plastic bag. I headed out, still unaware of the precise degree of my mediocrity, and found Liverpool.

After an inauspicious start, things gradually got worse. It didn't take me long to find that being broke and bored in a big city is only a soupçon less depressing than being bored and broke in the country. Oh, I know there are lots of free amusements, to use the term very loosely, in a place like Liverpool, especially when it's raining, which it seems to do thirteen months out of the year. There's the museum and the art gallery and the docks, to name but a few of the more deliriously exciting places, but museums and art galleries give me backache, and on the two occasions on which I availed myself of their therapy the silence and the smell of wet people only served to add to my depression and I walked out into the rain after ten minutes. The docks did little more for me. The sight of big liners hooting their way down the Mersey on voyages of romance to Canada or the United States or even the Isle of Man merely reminded me that I couldn't even afford the ferry across to New Brighton, so I stopped going there.

The job was at fault, of course. For the first twelve months I went stir-crazy in a nasty little box-room of an office off London Road which laughingly called itself the Liverpool Branch of G. Turner and Sons of London, Liverpool and Glasgow—Specialists in Removals. 'Moving house?—Don't worry and grouse! Let Turner's do it—You'll never rue it!' See what I mean? yes, well, I should have seen it, too, but before I came to my senses I'd been writing out invoices and inventories for almost a year and all the time wondering why I felt a hundred and forty years old.

That was five years ago and I've been with Wainwright's, the builders, since then. Oh, a lot of garbage has floated down the Mersey in five years, which, in retrospect, uncannily describes the passage of my life during that period. Well, perhaps not all garbage but certainly floaty. You know the old song—'Just Drifting and Dreaming'? That's about the size of it.

No, don't get me wrong. I'm not getting maudlin. I do have my cheerful moments and I had some pretty good times during those five years, and most of them came from cricket. Now, there's a game I love to play. Takes me right out of myself. You'd hardly credit the good times we've had in the pavilion when the rain has been sheeting down and we've got tired of watching the pitch disappearing under a foot of water. Really, some very good times.

Oh, and I did find a game I could play all by myself which gave me endless amusement. It is, perhaps, just a trifle inconvenient at times because it does require one to walk for miles and miles until one's feet throb and one's mind is attuned to thoughts of immediate suicide. It's called *Finding New Digs*. I spent hours playing it, searching the papers, bussing there, climbing stairs, smelling smells, frowning frowns, shaking heads, walking out, bussing back, sighing sighs, lighting fags, searching the papers, bussing there . . .

Which brings us back to Ravenscourt.

Mrs Barnes, her name is, the landlady. Auntie-figure. Short, pear-shaped, kindly but with a knowing eye. She 'suspects' me in a nice enough way just because I'm a man.

Husband Jack hasn't done a stroke of work in ten years. He sits in the front parlour all day long and reads the Bible. Nice enough fellow. Just smiles and nods; never says a dicky bird.

There's a young niece. Jean, her name is and she's sixteen and not at all bad looking. She's got a nice slim figure with a beautiful bottom, but she's a bit skinny on top. Never mind, they'll come. She's also got a lovely pair of eyes. They're a dark browny green and at times she looks a bit Chinese, which, particularly on her, is a very nice way to look. Jean lives upstairs with me.

To explain that, in case you're wondering, I got this room through a fellow at the cricket club, a fellow named Dennis and he also lives at Ravenscourt and he also lives with me, but, of course, we've all got our own rooms and they're right at the top of the house. Dennis, by the way, is a bit of a nutter but quite harmless. He's got red hair and laughs so much while he's telling you a joke that you never hear it, which is fine with me because I don't particularly like jokes.

Ravenscourt, as I said before, is a big place. It's got three floors, the ground floor and two more. At the bottom there are two generous receps., as the estate agents say, and the kitchen. On the first floor there are three bedrooms and the bathroom (Auntie and Jack live on this floor) and then on the top floor there are Jean's, Dennis's and my rooms and these are much smaller than the ones downstairs. Now, you might be asking yourself why does Auntie risk her sixteen-year-old niece up top with Dennis and me when she's got two other bedrooms to spare on the first floor. The answer is that Auntie is a business woman who could have Getty queuing for National Assistance the next morning if she ever got it into her head to take him over, and she is getting a very good rental indeed from two other lodgers for the downstairs rooms. And as far as any risk to Jean comes into it, there just isn't any, because Auntie creeps about the house, upstairs, downstairs, with the silent speed of a striking snake and very often frightens the hell out of us by popping on to the top landing a fifth of a second after we've heard her in the kitchen. You just can't trust that woman and she damn-well likes it that way.

Not that I'd ever try anything with Jean. I mean it would be entirely immoral, unethical and downright low to lech your landlady's niece on the premises and who the hell am I trying to kid. I get so bored sometimes up there in the crow's-nest that Auntie herself would do well to watch her step. Not really, but you know what I mean. A fellow's thoughts do tend to wander at times and they're not exactly helped by the sight of a sixteen-year-old lovely traipsing up from the bathroom all moist and cuddly from a hot bath and smelling like the soap counter at Boots, especially when her candlewick dressing gown is opening to her thighs as she climbs the stairs. Oh, she does that all right, and she knows to the square centimetre just how much thigh she's showing you, too. I reckon this kid feels her oats more times a week than the coalman's horse and she's just begging for the opportunity to sow them.

I remember one night about two months back. I'd been out on the razz with a couple of the lads from the club and I crept in about one in the morning with my shoes off. I managed to get up to the top floor without making a sound by walking on the edges of the stairs. When I got to the top, Jean's door was slightly open and her light was off. I opened my door and put

11

the light on and then I heard her whisper to me.

I pushed her door open a bit more and stood there looking at her and she was pretending to be asleep. Then she pretended to be dreaming and as she turned over she shook off the single sheet that had been covering her and she lay stretched out for me to see. She was wearing a white nylon nightie that was just about as opaque as a piece of clear cellophane and she was showing me the lot. I couldn't help smiling at the way she was going about it, but all the same she was very exciting and my mouth went as dry as a sawdust butty.

I took a couple of steps into her room and stood looking down at her. Oh, she was beautiful and she was driving me nuts. I couldn't resist her. I bent down and put my hand on her little breast and felt her nipple standing up like a cherry on a cup-cake. I gave her a kiss and she lay absolutely still for about ten seconds with her heart leaping around all over the place and then she pretended to wake up. She gave a lovely performance. She gasped and in a hoarse whisper asked me what I thought I was doing creeping into her room and attacking her like that. So I just grinned and kissed her again and she decided to stop acting and concentrate. Then we heard the click of the door on the landing below.

I shot into my room in two strides and began coughing as though I'd just woken up. I heard Auntie swishing up the stairs and go into Jean's room and I also heard Jean snoring away like a hippo with a noseful of seaweed. That kid could really act, I tell you.

Auntie gave me an extra suspicious stare the next morning, but she didn't say anything. I think she just made up her mind to double the guard in the future.

I've never had another opportunity to get at Jean since then, but she's always prick-teasing me, always saying things with at least three meanings and all of them suggestive; always showing me bits of herself as she comes out of her room, you know, like doing up the zip fly on her jeans or fastening the buttons on her blouse. I enjoy it, though. At least having her up there in the attic adds a little spice to life, even though we are doomed for ever to suffer physical frustration. And this is something all my other digs never had.

There are big drawbacks, though, at Ravenscourt, apart from Auntie. The room is too small and the view is quite depressing (Mathews' kitchen door, even on a sunny morning, can hardly be described even by the most undemanding as in-

12

spiring or uplifting) and there are just too many people in the house for one bathroom. There's always someone in there just when you're dying for a slash and half the time the water's cold. It's a depressing thought, but I'm afraid I'll have to start looking round again for another room.

You know, it really beats me why I can't see all these bad points in a place when I view it. It must be a kind of digs-drunkenness, a sort of hallucination that takes place that paints the prospect a rosier colour until you actually move in, and then, with your Y-fronts unpacked and stowed away in the top drawer, the scales are removed from your eyes and you see the dump as it really is. World-weariness is another way to describe it, I suppose. Huh, there I go again, getting all morbid, but the trouble really lies in the job I'm doing, not in the room. If life had any real meaning, if there was even a smidgin of dynamic interest in my daily grind I really wouldn't mind if my room overlooked a sewage plant. It wouldn't matter because I probably wouldn't even notice. That's the answer, of course. After five years at Wainwright's I'm still floundering around in a bog of disinterest. I'm up to my gizzard in invoices and statements and my mind is, as it has been for just too damned long, petrified by a mess of stultifying irrelevance. This life is not for me. I'm doing woman's work. I don't know what I ought to be doing, but I certainly know what I ought not to be doing.

Well, getting back to that Friday morning, these were the things that were nagging and depressing me as I went out on to the landing. And then it came to me, the sudden, overwhelming craving to change my job. I'd do it. I'd forget about changing rooms for a while and concentrate on finding the right job. Then, after that, I'd concentrate on finding just the right room.

The decision cheered me up no end. As I passed Jean's door, which was slightly open, I could hear her humming quietly to herself.

'Good morning, Russ,' she called. 'You're late.'

'Don't remind me,' I called back and stepped towards her door.

She heard my movement. 'Oh, don't come in! I'm not dressed.'

Her tone was pure provocation.

'I wouldn't dream of it,' I answered and peeped in.

13

She was standing in front of her long mirror, combing her shiny brown hair. She had her dressing gown on and it was wide open. Her slim body, as naked as a button, was thrust forward towards the mirror as she reached up to the back of her head and she was grinning herself silly knowing that I was looking at her.

She finished combing her hair and then, with a giggle, she brought the comb down and flicked her little brown pubic forest with it. She cocked her head to one side, inspecting the result like a West End hair stylist, nodded her satisfaction and put the comb down on the dressing table.

'There,' she said, as if I was half-way down the stairs, 'all ready for the new day.'

I roared with laughter and leapt down the stairs, nearly colliding with sneaky old Auntie who was leaping up them, her radar going berserk.

'Ah, Mr Tobin, thank Heaven you're up. I was just going to call you. My, you're late, aren't you? Didn't your alarm go off again? You really must get another clock, you know...'

She was still yacking when I closed the bathroom door.

TWO

When I got down to Wainwright's I was still feeling very cheerful, despite the soaking I'd got waiting for the bus. It's funny that, isn't it? When you're feeling excited about something, as I was about changing my job, nothing can really upset you. I'd had to wait nearly fifteen minutes in one of those open bus shelters and the wind had been blowing the rain in and generally behaving like it was first cousin to Hurricane Hazel and there was I smiling about life as if it was August Bank Holiday in Sidi Barrani.

Mind you, I still hadn't any idea what I was going to change my job to, but that didn't seem to matter for the time being. Just the thought of getting away from Wainwright's and office work was enough for now.

Not that Wainwright's is a bad place, as office jobs go. It's a construction company and a big one. They build all sorts of things like houses and bridges and things. The trouble is, we never get to see the end product, which is a pity because that's by far the most interesting side of the business. We do all the payments for stuff that Wainwright's buy and the wages for the men and that sort of thing, and we never see so much as a brick or a bag of cement because our office is entirely separate from the yards which are dotted about all over Liverpool. We're stuck down by the docks, not far from where the old overhead railway used to run. The offices themselves aren't bad, but the neighbourhood leaves a lot to be desired. Come to think of it, it stinks.

The view from practically all our windows is nil, because although we're quite close to the docks, we're surrounded on all sides by those towering, filthy old warehouses, so we don't even get a peep at the river or the boats to cheer life up a bit.

The office building itself is what is hilariously known as a 'temporary structure' and has been for the last ten years. It's built of breeze-block for cheapness and despite several coats of cream paint you still get the impression that you're slaving away in the new annexe of the Maginot Line. At any minute you expect the ten-inch guns to start up next door in the ladies' loo.

15

Ours is the biggest office in the building which is fortunate because we've got the most people. Sort of in charge of us is Bob Fitch. He's a tall, skinny bloke who looks like a cartoon drawing of De Gaulle except he's got a smaller nose. Old Fitch is all right. He lived most of his life in India and most of the time he's still out there. I feel sorry for a fellow like him. He must have had a marvellous life what with all that sun and chota pegs at the club and servants to bring him kippers in bed. And now this, Wainwright's down at the Liverpool docks and this everlasting rain.

He's a gentle man, Fitch; never really gets ruffled. Sometimes he has to bollock us for some grave misdemeanour like forgetting to change the nibs but he really couldn't give a damn. He's just hanging on now for retirement and then he'll probably just die of loneliness.

Mrs Reader, now, she's a very different proposition. She's a faggot. She's got the worst figure I've ever seen on a human being, man or woman. She's all hunched over somehow, and not through any deformity; it's just the way she carries herself. She's all bones and gristle and she's balmy to boot. Really! The way she carries on sometimes you'd think she'd just escaped from Rain Hill. She shouts and raves and waves her arms about one minute and then in the next she'll be laughing. A right nutter. When I first went there she decided to hate me just for fun and for the first week she really put me through the hoop. Then as was bound to happen with me, she came the old madam once too often and I told her to take a week off and do herself some mischief. She picked up a paper knife and for a minute I thought she was going to shout 'Ole!' and stick me, but then she fell about laughing and we've been like Freeman, Hardy and Willis ever since.

Then there's Mrs Robertson, but there's not very much I can say about her because she's never got anything to say about, or for, herself. She just sits in the corner and gets on with it. If Mrs Robertson says six words a day she's having a real knees-up. Nice but negative.

And at last I get to Gloria and don't I just wish I could, too. Glorious Gloria, I call her, and she certainly is. A nice, full-blooded blonde with a blouseful of breasts men dream about in their most private moments. She sits behind me and try as I might she will not change places.

But she's married, and there's the rub, if you know what I mean. We're just good mates and always it will be thus. Not

16

that that stops her from flirting, though. We've got one of those curious flirty office relationships which allows practically anything short of actual copulation to take place provided there are other people around. Then, the moment we're by ourselves, on the bus or in the cafe at lunchtime, it all seizes up as tight as a rusty bun until we've got an audience again, and then she's at it once more: teasing, suggestive, sometimes downright blatant like the time she backed me into a corner and unzipped my flies to prove to Mrs Reader that she wasn't chicken.

I'm sure she does fancy me on the quiet. I mean, no woman fools around like that unless she's attracted, does she? You wouldn't find Gloria with her hand on Bob Fitch's flies, for instance. Mind you, there's a thought. I'd love to see old Fitch backed up in a corner with those great charlies advancing on him and her fingers fumbling for his zip. I don't think he'd ever make retirement, somehow. He'd go out laughing his head off and there'd be nothing chota about his peg. I'll tell you. She really is some woman.

Well, that's the office staff. We do have an accountant who's in charge of all of us, but his office is down the corridor. He's a nasty piece of work. McFadden, his name is and he must be the fellow that started all this thing about Scotsmen being dour. He's the dourest bugger you'll meet in a very long hike over the heather. I think if he ever smiled his skin would split. He doesn't worry us too much though, because he always calls poor old Fitch into his office if he's got any complaints about us. But, his office is in a bad position—for us. We've got to pass his door to get into our office, and if we're late, as I was on that Friday, and his door is open, then he's got us, just like he got me that morning.

'Errrr ... Mrrrr Tobin!'

Blast! I thought I was going to make it.

'Good morning, Mr McFadden.'

He ignored the charm and looked at his watch as though it was a piece of smelly old gorgonzola.

'You've just arrrrived?' I could tell it wasn't a question, so there was no point in lying.

'I'm very sorry. It was the rain...'

He looked at me over his rimless glasses. 'What on earrrth has that to do with it?'

'Well ... it was my alarm clock. It didn't go off. I think it's rusty...'

'You mean the rain got into it. Where on earrrth do you sleep, man? In the back yard?'

I laughed heartily. 'No, of course...'

'Then, what do you mean?' He wasn't laughing heartily.

I shrugged. 'It didn't go off.'

The way he looked at me you'd think he'd just caught me coming out of the ladies' washroom.

'Then it must be faulty and must either be rrrepairred orrr rrreplaced immediately. This is Januarry, Mr Tobin, and not a verry auspicious way in which to starrrt the New Yearrr.'

He did go on, this bloke. I think his liver was still giving him jip from Hogmanay. All this fuss and I was only a quarter of an hour late.

'...if it happens again I'm verry much afrraid I shall have to rreporrt it to the Secrretarry.'

Huh, very much afraid. He'd have loved it. There, now d'you see why I'm so frustrated? A man shouldn't have to take this sort of nonsense from anybody, never mind this myopic Scottish twit. And it's all right people saying why don't you leave, then, but it just doesn't work that way. What guarantee is there that there won't be two McFaddens at the next place? Anyway, I'd had a bootful of this chap. He was talking to me as though I was a four-year-old who'd been playing hookey from Sunday school and things were bubbling up and fast coming to a head inside me, egged on, as it were, by my big decision that morning. If McFadden said one more thing, came out with one more insult...

'I'm afraid I shall have to keep a close eye on you, Tobin, and on your fellow worrkers in that office. The standard of worrk...'

That was it, the final insult. It was either resign right now or go on taking this garbage for the rest of my life.

'Well, you won't have to strain your eyesight watching me much longer, Mr McFadden,' I said, all nervous inside with temper. 'I'm resigning. I'll send you a letter.'

You'd think I'd kicked him in his sporran. His mouth dropped open like an asphyxiated goldfish and he spluttered all down his tie. I got out quick.

Well, I'd done it. I'd actually quit. But I don't think it really came home to me until I was in the cafe at lunchtime with Gloria.

Smokey Joe's is a real fatty sandwich of a place just round

18

the corner from Wainwright's. A lot of the dock lads go there and when we started going in, Gloria and I, there was a lot of leg-pulling at our expense. But this gradually subsided as the weeks went by and now we knew most of of the lads and had a good laugh with them. They still teased Gloria unmercifully, as you can guess, but it was all good clean stuff and she wasn't at all embarrassed. On the contrary, she lapped up all the attention like a thirsty cocker spaniel and smugly revelled in the knowledge that every one of the twenty or so men in there fancied her like mad. The place should really have been re-named Gloria's because she did more for the lads' comfort than Smokey Joe.

'What's on today?' she asked as we sat down.

'Sausages and mash or chef's special,' I said, reading the blackboard.

'I'm fed up with sausage and mash. I think I'll try the chef's special.'

We ordered two of them and then she leaned forward excitedly.

'Now, tell me all about it, Russ. What did you say to McFadden?'

Well, I elaborated a little, as men will when recounting their battle experiences to a lady, but I kept it within the bounds of credibility. She looked suitably impressed and proud of me but also a little worried.

'But, Russ, d'you think you should have given in your notice just like that ... before you get another job?'

I shrugged. 'I'm a great believer in timing, sweetie, and I think this was just the right time. It was a gift, wasn't it? You know how balmy I've been going down at Wainwright's for nearly five years now. And if I haven't quit during those five years, the chances are I wouldn't have quit in the next five. No, McFadden did me a big favour by being so rude.' I laughed. 'So did Mickey Mouse.'

She looked up and frowned. 'Who?'

'Mickey Mouse. He's on my alarm clock. You know, he walks in time with the ticking. I've had it since I was a kid.'

She nodded. 'Yes, I know. I had one, one time, but I pulled his legs off.' She frowned again. 'How could he be rude to you?'

I laughed at her. 'No, he wasn't rude. He just made me late this morning. I think he's got rusty bells.'

'Rusty what?'

'Bells!'

She was grinning. She knew I'd said bells.

Smokey Joe came up with two chef's specials and when he'd gone, Gloria peered at the plate and said, 'What on earth is it?'

I tasted it. 'I think it's sausage meat and mash.'

'Oh, that's nice,' she said. 'Makes a change, doesn't it?'

We ate for a while and chatted about this and that, and then she said, 'But what are you going to do, Russ ... about a job?'

I shrugged. 'I don't know yet, but I'm not going back into an office. It's living death for me. I get so frustrated I can't think straight.'

She pushed her plate aside and sipped her tea. 'What else is there? What experience have you got?'

I grinned at her and she said, 'Oh, not that. You're probably a genius at that, but it won't buy groceries.'

'Gigolos manage to eat,' I said, teasing her.

She laughed. 'Oh, yes, I could just see you plucking a seventy-year-old bird for three square meals a day, I don't think.'

'Please,' I joked, 'you're spoiling my lunch.'

'Well then?'

I shrugged again. 'I just don't know, Gloria. I was born in the country, but I don't fancy farming—I'm just no good first thing in the morning. I wouldn't mind working all day and into the evening, but I'm just no good in the early morning.'

She finished her tea and dabbed at her lips with a paper serviette. 'Well, what about...' she sighed, '...no, that wouldn't do either.'

'What?'

I offered her a cigarette.

'I was going to suggest the forces, but they're very early morning, aren't they?'

I shuddered. 'My God, can you imagine getting a sergeant like McFadden over you and not being able to get from under for five years?'

I lit the cigarettes and we smoked in silence while we racked our brains.

'Selling?' she said.

I looked up and considered the word, then shook my head.

'Why not, Russ? At least you wouldn't have to start work at

the crack of dawn.'

I shook my head. 'No, it's not me, is it?'

She laughed as if I'd said something ridiculous. 'Why on earth not? You've got the looks, you're intelligent . . .'

'Go on!' I joked.

'No, really, Russ. I think you'd make a marvellous salesman —especially if you sold to women.'

'Eh?'

She sighed. 'You know, you really do underestimate yourself, don't you? You're a very good looking man. One look at those baby blue eyes of yours and the women will be down on their knees begging you to take their money . . .' she grinned a big sexy grin, '. . . and everything else they've got, too.'

Now, perhaps you won't believe this, but suddenly I felt shy. Here she was saying the nicest things, things a man loves to hear from a woman, and she was really meaning them, not just trying to help me make my mind up, and she was making me blush.

She saw it, too, and laughed at me in a nice way. 'And if you blush like that at them, they'll never let you off the premises.'

For a minute we didn't say anything while the thought sank into my noodle. Selling. Well. it was certainly a possibility. If I worked it right I'd be pretty well my own boss and perhaps I could choose my own hours.

'I'd need a car,' I said, almost to myself.

Gloria sighed and shook her head. 'There you go, finding problems already. Some firms provide cars, don't they?'

I nodded. 'Yes, some do.'

'Well, then.'

I thought about it a bit more and then said, 'What could I sell?'

'Oh, there're hundreds of things, Russ. And once you learn how to sell, it doesn't really matter what the product is, does it? Just as long as you like it.'

I put my hand on hers and gave it a squeeze. 'You are marvellous, pet. Really, you are a very good mate.'

She smiled and wiggled her nose. 'Go on with you.'

She looked at her watch and gasped. 'Oh, Lord, look at the time. We've got to fly! McFadden will be wetting himself.'

I paid for the lunches as a small thank you to Gloria and we walked out to the street. On the way back we had to pass a small alley-way, and as we approached it I got hold of Gloria's

21

arm and slowed her down.

I looked up and down the street and then led her into the alley. She was smiling at me, knowing what I was going to do, and she went willingly.

I put my arms around her and brought her close to me and she slipped her hands inside my coat and pulled me even closer. Oh, my word, what a handful of woman she was. I could feel her lovely breasts sticking into me and her hips began massaging mine like a pair of warm, soft hands and doing the most diabolical things to Frederick the Great. I kissed her, a little one at first, but then she took over and damn-near swallowed me. After a bit she pulled away and looked up at me with a smouldering, dreamy look in her eyes. 'Good luck, Russ. You're going to do very well, I just know it. You may not sell many vacuum cleaners, but, by gum, you're going to make an awful lot of women happy.'

I laughed at her and she gave me a little peck on the mouth. 'It's a pity I'm married,' she murmured. 'You could sell me this any day of the week.'

She pushed her tummy against Frederick, which now was spoiling the cut of my jacket up by the breast pocket.

'No charge to old friends,' I gulped.

'We'll see,' she said naughtily. 'I've fancied you ever since I came to the office, but I wouldn't let anything happen while we were working together. But now . . .'

I gulped again. 'What about your husband?'

She looked suddenly sad. 'We're separating, Russ. He's got somebody else.'

'Oh, I'm sorry,' I said, a little untruthfully.

She shrugged and smiled. 'Keep in touch, Russ. I may need a new vacuum cleaner before long.'

I kissed her on the forehead. 'You can count on it.'

All that afternoon and all the way home on the bus I thought of nothing else but selling. Mind you, I've got a pretty ludicrous imagination and you'd hardly credit the things I saw myself doing. I was up at Buckingham Palace receiving a medal from Her Majesty for being top insurance salesman in the country for the tenth year running; I was lecturing at the Institute of Directors on The Art of Overcoming the Impossible in Selling; I was taking delivery of my new Rolls Silver Cloud and then whipping around in it and selling fifty washing machines in one afternoon just to celebrate. Pretty daft, really, but I am a bit inclined to daydream like that.

By the time I got home I was convinced that Gloria was right. Selling was for me.

I said such a cheery hello to Auntie Barnes in the hallway that she gave me an extra suspicious glare and I could sense her getting her mental running shoes on to follow me upstairs.

Jean's door was wide open and she was sitting on the bed painting her toenails.

'Hi,' she said, not looking up.

She had on a white transparent blouse and the tightest, thinnest jeans you've ever seen. With one knee cocked up to her chin she was leaving nothing of her delectable anatomy to my ludicrous imagination.

I leaned in the doorway and kept an ear open for Auntie.

'How are you?' I asked.

'Starving,' she muttered into her kneecap.

I shoved myself off the doorpost and went into my room. In the top drawer of the tallboy I'd been keeping a bar of chocolate in case I got too lazy one night to go out for dinner. I threw it on to her bed from the doorway and she jerked up in delighted surprise.

'You're an angel!'

'Don't pay me now—later will do,' I joked.

She grinned and threw the wrapper at me and bit off a couple of pieces.

'Want some?' she asked, holding the bar out.

'Not chocolate. Offering anything else?'

She squirmed and brought both knees up to her chin, showing me even more of her anatomy.

'I'll tell Auntie if you persist in making improper suggestions,' she said.

'It'll be your whatsit . . . word against mine.'

She giggled and continued to eat.

'I'm changing my job,' I said nonchalantly, as if the president of I.C.I. had been pestering me again and I'd finally agreed.

'Oh?'

I'd heard more enthusiasm in a dentist's waiting room.

'I'm going to be a salesman.'

She choked on the chocolate. 'You're what?'

'I'm taking up a selling career,' I said with dignity.

She laughed rudely and I could have hit her. This was doing my ego no good at all. Could Gloria have been wrong?

'Provided you're selling pound notes at a bob each you should do very well,' she laughed.

'Ha ha ha, you kill me.'

This was ridiculous. This ... this child didn't know her pubic bone from a radiator cap. What the heck did she know about selling—or salesmen.

'Try and sell me something,' she said haughtily.

'I already have,' I said quietly. 'And if your aunt hadn't come up, you'd have bought it, too.'

She went very quiet and a little smile tickled her lips. I knew I'd got her. She couldn't deny that she wanted it and if that isn't salesmanship, just tell me what is. Gloria was right. Have faith in your product and you can't go wrong. Well, I was carrying my commodity around with me—sex appeal, and all I had to do now was decide what secondary line to carry—fridges or vacuum cleaners or encyclopaedias. I suddenly felt very excited. I had an overwhelming feeling that I was going to do very well in this selling game. What was the old adage I'd heard time and time again? Sell yourself first and the rest is easy. I wonder if the fellow who first said it really meant it so literally?

THREE

I don't know whether you've ever tried to find a job from the papers, particularly a selling job, but if you have, you'll know it's a pretty frustrating business. A lot of these firms are so cocksure of themselves that they don't even say what they're selling. We're all supposed to know or not care because of the honour of working for them or something. And then there's the other reason, of course, that their product is too personal (and that usually means too embarrassing) to put in print either from a good-taste point of view or because they know they'd never get a salesman in a billion years if they did state their product. Things like, well, you know, all the doodads that come under the enigmatic heading of 'toilet requisites'.

I wasted one whole morning of my precious life answering one of these jokers and even after talking to the managing director for ten minutes I still didn't have the vaguest idea what he was selling. Eventually he got around to it after a big build-up about prospects for the future and all that twaddle and then I realized why he'd been prevaricating all over the place. He was selling funerals on easy terms!

Well, I mean to say, who in his right mind is going to knock on a door and say, 'Good morning, madam, with our help you could die on H.P.'

No wonder the poor fellow looked a bit down in the mouth; he's had the ad. in the *Echo* for months. He'll be lucky. Oh, I know people do save up for their funerals and very sensibly, too, but it's done by the insurance companies in a much more subtle way, isn't it? They don't come right out and say if you want chrome-plate instead of brass on the box you'd better ante-up on the premiums. They do it so nicely and emphasize one's obligations to dependants and all that. Now, there's a line you can sell. But it's a far cry from trying to convince some young bird in curlers that over the centuries granite is so much more durable than the cheaper sandstone job. I do wish these people would be more honest in their advertising, it would save an awful lot of one's time.

And then there's the other sneaky bunch. They get you all excited about earning fifteen thousand a year if you've just got the right go go go! and then they slip it to you gently that you've got to provide your own car, your own contacts, and you've got to buy all the stock from them first before you sell it! Oh, I tell you, you wouldn't credit the nerve of some of them. One little merchant named Mahatma Isaacson even offered to keep back fifty per cent of our commission in case we ran into hard times. He promised to keep it safely in his bank account and we could draw it out if our earnings dropped below the national average four weeks running.

Well, I was getting a bit down in the mouth about all this, I can tell you. Most of these appointments I was having to do in the evenings because I was still working out my month's notice at Wainwright's and after a day in the office and then traipsing all over town in the evening, I was getting very fed up.

Then, who should come to the rescue but Dennis, the fellow on the top floor with me at Ravenscourt. I was telling him my troubles over a quiet *Double Diamond* in our local and he suddenly went into a deep think.

'Oh, now who is it in the cricket club that's in that line...' He scratched his head and drank some beer and then he had it. 'Ah, chap in the first eleven—Jim Stanford. Sells sewing machines. Does very well apparently.'

My hopes dropped again. 'Sewing machines?'

I scratched my head and drank some beer, too.

'Why not?' asked Dennis.

I laughed. 'Well, I mean...'

Well, why not sewing machines?

'I don't know why not,' I said. 'Just seemed funny for a minute. It's something I'd never thought about.'

Dennis finished his beer and got up for two more. When he brought them back, he said. 'Should be a good line, you know, Russ. The women in this country are pretty industrious, aren't they? They do a lot of sewing for kids and things.'

I nodded thoughtfully. 'I suppose so. I don't know about the young ones but my mother and all her friends had one when I was a lad—a sewing machine, I mean.'

Dennis nodded sagely. 'Oh, I shouldn't have thought there's all that much money around even today that young wives and mothers can afford to chuck things away and buy new ones instead of mending them.'

Dennis isn't twenty yet but he manages to sound like the Minister for Economic Affairs at times. Still, he had a point.

'I'll think about it,' I said, pouring the beer.

'Can't do any harm, can it?' he said. 'Have a word with Jim Stanford on Saturday.'

Came Saturday.

Slash Lane Cricket Club is a Green Shield stamp of grass completely surrounded by the gaunt and sooty four-storeyed remnants of a by-gone affluent age. It's a district of silent groves and crescents that meander around and double back on themselves like a cow's intestines, designed, one supposes, to confuse the stranger who inadvertently wandered in and to encourage him to wander out again.

These were the town houses of the wealthy Liverpool merchants when Victoriana was mod. gear. They are massive affairs with lofty rooms and ornate ceilings; long, shuttered bay windows which once looked out on to small but elegant grounds, tended, no doubt, by gardeners who permanently had the fingers of one hand plucking at a subservient forelock. The grand life.

Now, ghosts walk and whisper along the crummy, gas-lit streets at night and peep from behind the dirty privet hedges, hearing but refusing to hear the low-bred voices that ring through the cavernous hallways and down the crumbling stairs.

'Nellie! Where's me bluddy underpants?'

'You's'll find them in the bleedin' drawer if you'd use your bluddy eyes!'

The great, grey manors are now all flats and the proletariat have moved in. The once-proud gardens are sad, mossy, weedy receptacles for untold tons of assorted garbage, and under cover of the rain, the trees cry.

Slash Lane itself is merely a cinder track running the length of the cricket ground. It leads nowhere but gives us access to the club. Why it's called Slash Lane no one seems to know, but the rusty corrugated iron fence is a favourite place for dogs to cock their legs and that seems to be as good a reason as any.

Now, you may be wondering what I was doing at the cricket club in the middle of winter, so I'd better put that straight. You see, it's a very comprehensive club and far more than just a cricket club. We've got tennis courts and a bowling green and lots of indoor facilities, too. The clubhouse is really quite something. It's a permanent brick-built job with showers and dressing rooms and a good bar. There are two full-size snooker tables and dart boards and a piano and even a small stage for

27

concert parties, and the place is open all year round. It's more of a social club, you see, which is nice because this way you keep in touch with the lads during the eleven months and three weeks of the year when it's either too cold or too wet to play cricket.

I'd got Jim Stanford's telephone number from the club secretary and we'd arranged to meet on Saturday night for a game of snooker and a beer. I did know him, slightly, but as he was in the first eleven and I was very firmly in the second, we hadn't actually chatted before. But he'd seemed a nice bloke on the phone and I was looking forward to meeting him.

It was about eight o'clock when I walked into the club. The place was beginning to warm up. Old Joe Hendrix was thumping away on the piano, thoroughly enjoying himself, and there were lots of pint glasses dotted around the room. The two dart boards were taking a lot of punishment and the snooker balls were knocking one another silly on the tables.

Jim Stanford was propping the bar up and was being bored stupid by Old Man Croutch who was obviously telling him how he copped all ten wickets against the Gas Works in 1902. Stanford's relief when he saw me was profound. He nodded an apology to Croutch and came to meet me.

'Hello, Russ. What are you having?'

'I'll have a light ale, Jim.'

He wasn't very tall, Stanford, but he was athletic-looking and he had a good face. It wasn't difficult to see why he was successful at selling. His smile was genuine and his handshake was warm but not overpowering. You felt you could trust him and that what he had to say was worth listening to.

Old Croutch moved off to bore someone else and we moved up to the bar.

Stanford ordered the beers and said, 'I've put our names down for snooker, Russ. We should be on soon. Table two's nearly finished.'

'I'm not much good,' I said.

'Me neither.'

We drank some beer and went to sit down by table two. When we'd settled in a bit, he said, 'So you're interested in selling?'

I nodded. 'Yes, I think so. I know that sounds indefinite but I'm not sure yet. All I know is that I'm bored potty doing what I am doing and I've just got to change.'

He grinned. 'What's that?'

28

'Office work.'

He snorted. 'Don't tell me. I had a couple of years in a bank and used to wake up screaming.'

The pink ball rocketed into the top pocket and I thought the clubhouse was going to fall down. It was Owen, the fast bowler of the first eleven who had put it there and the big-headed sod was smirking all over his face. Nobody liked Owen. He was a rude bastard but somehow he managed to get wickets so they put up with him. He was playing snooker with the captain of the first eleven and narrowly losing to him.

'Fifty to my fifty-four,' said the captain, shifting the score board. 'You need the black to win.'

Owen glowered at the black as if he was trying to frighten it into the hole and then he got down on his honkers and studied the angles like Joe Davis.

'Watch the big finish,' said Stanford through the side of his mouth. He obviously liked Owen as much as I did.

Owen stretched across the table to the white ball and slammed his cue at it in a grand coup. The black streaked from the white across the baize and disappeared into the bottom pocket. For a moment Owen remained frozen, overcome with self-satisfaction and quite unaware that the white was rolling slowly but inexorably towards the middle pocket for a foul.

'And that makes me two games and five bob up, skipper,' Owen said snidely.

Plock! The white kissed the cush and fell down the well. It had been worth coming to the club just to see Big Head's face.

'Shite,' he said.

The skipper gave himself four on the board and coolly doubled the black into the bottom pocket to win. They wandered off to the bar and Stanford and I started racking up the balls.

'You should do well at selling,' Jim said. 'You've got the right image—plenty of personality, good looks...'

'Thanks,' I said, really beginning to believe it now.

He tossed a shilling and I called tails and won.

'You break,' I said.

He put the white neatly behind the triangle of reds without disturbing them more than a sixteenth of an inch.

'Thought you couldn't play,' I said.

'Fluke,' he laughed.

I never could play the subtle game so I smashed them up

and scattered the reds all over the table. Not one dropped.

'Sewing machines are a good line,' he said, putting down an easy red. 'Once you get to know them intimately you can do a really good demonstration. They're very impressive, you see, because they do impressive things. Blue.' He drove the blue into the middle pocket and I replaced it on the centre spot.

'Now you take a vacuum cleaner. What can you really do with a cleaner? Clean, that's all. There's no challenge there for a woman. She just runs the thing up and down the carpet and that's it. There's nothing there to excite her imagination.'

He cut in another red from an impossible angle and brought the white dead on to the black, then he floated the black in with the touch of a brain surgeon probing for buckshot.

'But with a sewing machine you can paint pictures. Think of all the attachments, Russ—the pleater, the quilter, the button-holer, the hemmer. All very impressive gadgets that make professional results possible to even the dumbest housewife—or so she thinks.'

He didn't speak again until he'd slammed down two more reds and a pink.

'I've sold quite a few of the household appliances, Russ, but there's nothing to beat sewing machines. None of the others give you the personal contact in the home, you see. Fridges, stoves, T.V.s—they've got to be sold in the shop really. You can't go door to door with a fridge on your back, can you? And I don't go for store selling. Get the little darlings in the privacy of their own homes where they feel safe and comfortable and half the battle's over.'

He cut in an incredible brown and tickled another red down the centre pocket which must have seemed to him as wide as the mouth of a three gallon bucket.

'And you see, when we knock on the front door, the woman really does want to buy a sewing machine—that's the beauty of the system. It isn't cold canvassing, God, no, that's really for idiots. We advertise our machine in the papers, you see, and they send in a coupon asking for a dem, so they're expecting us when we knock on the door.'

'Sounds too good to be true,' I said, trying to keep track of his score.

He smiled. 'Ah, well, there's a bit of a catch to it. It's what is known as "switch selling" in the trade. Oh, it's quite honest and above board, although ... er ... some might regard it as a fraction unethical ... damn!'

He missed a yellow by the thickness of a fag paper and it was my turn. I muffed an easy red, possibly through not having played for so long, and then it was his turn again. He didn't muff the red, nor the black after it.

'You see,' he went on, 'we advertise a small, cheap machine which really is very good value for the money, and usually the customer buys it straight away because that's what she's sent the coupon in for. Well, when that little transaction is completed, we tell them that we get paid a commission to demonstrate a much better machine so that they can tell their friends about it. So off we dash back to the car and haul in this other machine. Ha, you should see their faces when they clap eyes on this one and compare it to the one they've just bought. It's as different as a gum drop to a bum boil. Talk about a Rolls-Royce and a roller skate! Well, their eyes pop out and you can hear them "oo-ing and aah-ing" behind you and telling you in the same breath that they could never afford that. And you turn round and say you wouldn't want to buy it anyway, madam, would you, because you've just bought this? Then you pick her little mess of maggots up and rattle it around as if it was something out of a Corn Flakes packet. Then you start the dem.

'Well, by the time you've told them about the non-existent special offer that's on for just that week which cuts the price to shreds and includes five quid's worth of attachments and free sewing lessons, they're going weak at the knees. Then you bring out your H.P. card and tell them that by pure co-incidence the down payment is exactly what they've paid you for the cheap machine and the monthly payments they can easily make up by saving on new clothes. It's a cinch, Russ, a cinch.'

I wasn't sure whether he meant the sale or the blue at the top of the table which he trebled into the centre pocket. But he certainly made the sewing machine business sound easy and exciting.

'How many do you sell a week?' I asked, putting up the blue.

'An average of ten,' he said nonchalantly. 'At a fiver a time.'

I whistled. 'Fifty a week?'

He nodded and put the last red down.

'On average,' he said, chalking his cue and eyeing the pink. 'Sometimes I do seventy quid, other weeks only thirty or so.

It's a bit seasonal. The winter's the best time when the girls are stuck in the house. I made sixty-five this week.'

He blasted the pink and then prodded in the yellow.

'Do you need a car?' I asked.

'Yes, you do, but the firm doesn't specify a Lincoln Continental. Any presentable old banger will do.'

The green, brown, blue, pink and black shot into the pockets as though they were attached by elastic and the game finished at something like thirteen thousand to nil.

I shook my head when Stanford suggested another game and we went to the bar for another beer. As loser I paid the barman for the game and then we took our drinks to a small table across the room.

'You haven't got a car?' said Stanford.

I shook my head. 'Not at fifteen quid a week.'

He looked aghast. 'Is that all you're knocking up, fifteen quid?'

I shrugged. 'You know what office work pays.'

'Too true. It was the same at the bank. You pay dearly for security, don't you? I never could see the sense of living in virtual poverty just to retire on a scrap of pension which you probably wouldn't live to enjoy anyway. Russ, you'll have to do better than that, mate. Fifteen quid is disgusting.'

'How do you really think I'd do on sewing machines?' I asked.

He drank some beer and offered me a fag.

'Russ,' he said quietly, 'we've got men working for us who haven't got half your looks or personality—no, I'm not shooting you the s.h.one t.—really, they're pretty ordinary fellows but they're selling their half dozen a week regularly. Look at it this way. All right, we sell only on commission—no salary— but the firm does a lot of advertising to compensate for that. Every day we get four leads each. Now, if we only sell twenty-five per cent that's one sale a day and maybe two on Saturdays. There's your thirty or thirty-five quid a week. And I reckon you could do much better than that. You could be on forty quid a week in no time, once you've got the hang of it.'

I was really getting excited about it now. 'How do I start, Jim?'

'I'll have a word with the boss. There are two partners, Jimmy Sands and Allen Draper—Sands is the brains, Draper has the capital. Maybe Sands would let you work in the shop until you get a car. How are you fixed for cash?'

'I could raise fifty pounds. I've got some Savings Bonds.'

Stanford thought for a moment. 'We might be able to help you there, too. The company's got an arrangement with a local garage and all the lads take their cars there for servicing. We get a cheap rate. Maybe he could find a reliable banger for you for fifty down. Anyway, leave it to me. I'll have a chat with them and see what they can do.'

'It's very good of you, Jim . . .'

He waved his hand. 'Nuts. I got help to get out of the bank so I'm passing it on. I know what you're going through in that office. By the way, have you given your notice in yet?'

I nodded. 'Yes, I couldn't stand it any longer. I've got one more week to go.'

Stanford grinned. 'Then we'll have to get cracking. We can't have you out of work, can we?'

FOUR

During Sunday I got very steamed up about the new job. I'd dreamt about it on Saturday night and I woke up on Sunday morning impatient to see Sands and get started.

I went down to breakfast in a very good mood and chatted old Auntie about this and that until I could see her backing away from the sheer weight of verbiage. I didn't mention selling sewing machines, though, just in case she objected to me doing a job like that. I didn't want to have to find a new room as well as a new job.

And I didn't tell Jean either not about the machines, because I knew she'd be snide about them and make inane remarks that would get up my jacket and make me lose my temper. And life was just too good to let that happen. So I just kept it all bottled up until Monday and let rip at lunchtime when I had Gloria alone in the restaurant.

She is a good kid, you know. She got as excited for me as I was for myself. Her eyes were shining like a Nigerian's cuff in a coal box and she was grinning to beat the band.

'Oh, Russ, I think that's a good idea. That Jim Stanford's right, you know. I'm sure you could do very well at that.'

I grinned back at her, getting more confident all the time. 'What makes you think so?'

'Well, it's as I said the other day. I don't think you can go wrong selling to women and sewing machines are the very thing. They're pure female merchandise, aren't they? What more could you ask for? You go to the house by appointment, so you're not barging your way in, and you've got an interesting appliance to demonstrate. I think you'll sell a million.'

She was leaning forward, close to me, and I could smell her perfume. I wanted to get hold of her and kiss her.

'How are you off for a sewing machine?' I murmured.

Her eyes went all soft and passionate and my heart started thumping around my chest again.

'I told you, you could sell me anything,' she said in a low, husky voice. 'And after next week-end you can come round and give me a demonstration any time.'

'Next week-end?' I had to cough to get the lumps out of my throat.

She nodded. 'I had a good straight talk with my husband yesterday. He's moving out next Saturday. We just can't go on like this. He admits he's got someone else but until yesterday we'd never talked about it—just let things drift. Now he's decided and I'm keeping the flat.'

There was a little silence between us and then I said, 'He must be mad, Gloria.'

She smiled and shrugged. 'It went stale a long time ago, Russ. We've been married five years but it went wonky after three. It's been a big mistake to hang on for the other two.'

She cheered up suddenly because that's the kind of girl she is; she doesn't like making people uncomfortable. The warmth came back into her eyes and the lumps came back into my throat.

'You'd be very good for me, Russ. Oh, nothing so drastic as marriage, I'm not proposing to you, but I like you and I need you and I want you.' She smiled, a little shy smile. 'You'd be shocked at the thoughts I have about you sometimes.'

Well, how about that for honesty? But that's what a man gets from a mature woman and it's pretty nice. This is what I've heard other men talking about. Once you've had an experienced woman, they've said, you've just got no time for the other sort. Well, think about Jean upstairs with her teasing and giggling and messing about. Can you hear Jean saying what Gloria just said? I'm sure I can't.

I had to concentrate to get my voice under control and stop my legs shaking and then I said, 'I don't even know where you live.'

She dipped into her handbag and handed me a piece of paper. 'It's in Childwall.'

I put the address and telephone number carefully in my top pocket.

'You'll be my very first customer,' I said.

'I'll take an awful lot of persuading,' she said, her eyes dancing all over me. 'You may have to come several times.'

'But I'll get you in the end,' I croaked.

'Yes, please do,' she said.

The call I expected from Jim Stanford telling me he'd fixed up an appointment with Sands didn't come, and by Tuesday afternoon a panic started inside me that just wouldn't be talked away. I began conjuring up all sorts of reasons why he hadn't called and not one of them was optimistic. Obviously, I thought, Jimmy Sands had refused to see me because I'd had no experience or because I hadn't got a car or because he didn't want any more salesmen. I even thought that Jim Stanford had been knocked down on the way to work on Monday morning and was lying in a coma in some hospital. Crazy, I know, but it was Tuesday afternoon and something should have happened by now.

Five o'clock came and still no news. I said goodnight to the office and grabbed my mac off the hook. To make things worse it was raining again and I got soaked waiting for a bus.

By the time I got home I was feeling pretty depressed and I was so full of myself as I opened the front door that I didn't hear the honking behind me. After the third or fourth toot I looked around and there was Stanford sitting in his car by the kerb.

I leapt down the steps and ran over to him and jumped into the passenger seat. It was still chucking it down and his wipers were going balmy but now I didn't mind being soaked to the skin.

'Hello, Russ,' he said. 'Christ, you're wet.'

'Hi, Jim. How did it go?'

'Sorry I couldn't phone you earlier but Sands has been down South. I had a word with him this afternoon and he'd like to see you at six tomorrow evening. I told him you were still working and it might be difficult for you to get off so he said pop round after work.'

'Jim, thanks a million . . .' I said excitedly.

He waved his hand at me. 'Forget it. I hope you can make it, Russ. Don't be nervous of Sands. He puts on a bit of an act with the new fellows but it's only to test them. Just stand up to him and you'll get along fine. He s only trying to find out if you're tough enough for the business. Just stay calm and look after yourself.'

'Thanks for the advice.'

He looked at his watch. 'I'll have to go, I've got an appointment. Rule one, never be late for an appointment. I'll see you, Russ. Give me a call tomorrow night and let me know how you got on.'

'I will, Jim, certainly.'

I put my hand on the door to get out.

'Oh,' he said, 'I've had a word with the garage chap. If you join us he thinks he may be able to do something for you. He's got a Hillman coming in in a couple of weeks that he could let you have for a hundred and fifty. He could do it for fifty down and fix up the insurance for you, too.'

'Marvellous, Jim. Thanks very much. I really do mean it.'

I stood on the front steps and watched his new Consul slide round the corner. Six o'clock tomorrow night. Twenty-four of the longest hours of my life to go.

Wednesday morning.

Gloria wolf-whistled me when I went in to the office. All the others just stared and even Mrs Reader was stuck for a rude remark.

'I say,' said Gloria in a posh accent. 'Whom 'ave we 'eare?' She looked through the holes in her scissors like a Dowager Duchess peering through her pince-nez. 'Can it be the Rt. Hon. Russell Tobin Esquire?'

'More like his dog's dinner,' said Mrs Reader, recovering her rapier wit.

I must say I did look pretty good. I had on my best blue serge which was as slim-line as they come and the creases in the trousers were cutting my knee-caps off. My shirt was whiter than white and the slim blue Italian silk tie had cost me half a week's pocket money only a fortnight before. Add to that little lot a pair of soft leather casuals on the feet and you've got a pretty sexy-looking creature.

I could see Gloria was really impressed. She gave a funny sort of squirm and goose pimples came out on her arms. She gave me a big wink and said, 'I'll take six of whatever you're selling,' which was very much our own private joke.

'Going for an interview?' Bob Fitch asked politely.

'I didn't know the Prime Minister was resigning,' cackled Mrs Reader. 'You takin' over?'

'Sssh!' I said. 'The poor fellow doesn't know yet. The shock would kill him.'

And so it went on all day. I wouldn't tell them anything, though, and Mrs Reader was beside herself with curiosity, but it was a bit late in the day for her tantrums. Gloria and I drove her potty with little looks and whisperings and towards the end of the afternoon I thought she was going to set fire to herself with frustration. Well, it served the old crab right for what she'd done to me in the past.

At lunchtime I couldn't stand the ragging I knew I'd get from the lads in Smokey Joe's so Gloria went out for sandwiches and some tea and brought them back to the office.

Then, one by one the others left and we had the place to ourselves. For the first time since we'd known each other we were completely alone. Gloria was just as aware of it as I was and she was enjoying every second of it. She sat demurely behind her desk and nibbled at a sandwich but I could tell from her eyes that her mind most certainly wasn't on spam and salad.

'Did I tell you that you look ravishing today?' she said into her sandwich.

'Not in as many words.'

'Well, you do.'

'Thank you, ma'am.'

'And you're doing the most awful things to my innerds.'

'Oh?'

'You've given me stomach ache all morning.'

I moved behind her and put my hands on her shoulders. She had on a pretty and very sheer nylon blouse and her skin felt so good through it. It was silky soft and warm. I could feel a tremor running through her. She breathed deeply to ease the shaking and from where I stood I could see her magnificent breasts swell like inflating balloons inside her brassiere. I couldn't resist them. With a quick flick I opened the top two buttons and slipped my hand inside. She breathed out quickly to make room for me and then I was there. I'd waited two years to do this. Her breast was as soft and warm as a Labrador puppy and the nipple was standing out rock-hard as a thimble. She moaned softly and pressed my hand hard.

'Squeeze!' she said suddenly. 'Hurt me!'

I laid on the pressure and nipped her nipple between my thumb and forefinger and I thought she was going to pass out. Her head rolled back against my stomach and her eyes were tight closed. Her mouth opened and she started to make gasping noises as though she was choking.

Then, suddenly, she reached up for my other hand and pulled it down sharply towards her thighs which were now wide open. Oh, if only this was some place other than the office. My hand touched the silky top of her stocking and then her flesh, flesh that was hotter than I'd ever thought flesh could be.

'Oh, Russ ... Russ ...' she was moaning.

Then we heard the footsteps in the corridor and Mrs Reader's fortunate cackle. I sprang away from Gloria and put as much distance between us as I could get before the door opened. When they came in I was tidying out my top drawer.

All afternoon I couldn't take my mind off Gloria and her craving. Oh, what the future held. Occasionally I would look around at her on some pretext or other and I'd see the future right there in her eyes. They glowed like the ignited touchpaper of a giant firework and promised just as big a bang.

At five o'clock I threw her a big kiss and she wished me good luck, all of which had Mrs Reader coming out in pimples again because she didn't know what we were talking about.

I was on pins at the bus stop because the queue was twice as long as it normally was and the buses seemed fewer, but I got to one eventually and got into town in good time.

I had no trouble finding the Ritebuy Sewing Machine shop; it was just off the main shopping centre, tucked round the corner where the rents are a bit cheaper. As I had a couple of minutes to spare I walked past it a few times on the opposite side of the road, just to get the feel of the place.

It was a good-looking shop; it looked clean and efficient. The double windows were dressed well with the different models of machines—portable and cabinets and so on—and coloured materials had been draped around to fancy it all up a bit. There was a girl dummy there who was dressed in a pretty frock and she was saying, with the aid of a card, look what I made for myself with a Ritebuy Sewing Machine and only six lessons. It all looked very convincing.

Next to the shop was an alleyway which obviously led round the back of the building, and while I was watching, a small van came out and turned towards town. On the side of the van it said: RITEBUY SEWING MACHINES—PROMPT AFTER-SALE SERVICE. The driver was a dreamy-looking youth who was driving with one hand and clicking his fingers to some wild beat that must have been emanating from a transistor which dangled from his rear-view mirror and effectively obscured about a fifth of his windshield.

I checked my watch. It was one minute to six. I crossed the road and went into the shop.

A suave-looking fellow in an expensive suit floated across and gave me a full broadside of very white teeth. There was the air of a playboy about him and there was no denying his charm.

'Good afternoon, sir. May we be of service?'

He had a good voice, too. Very dolce vita.

'My name is Tobin,' I said, giving him back the teeth. 'I have an appointment with Mr Sands.'

My name registered but I'll give him this, the charm didn't diminish one millimetre.

'Ah, Mr Tobin—of course! How do you do? My name is Allen Draper. I'm Mr Sands' partner.'

Well, now, this was a good start.

'I'll just check that Mr Sands is free,' he said, sweeping away towards the back of the shop to a glass door which said 'Private'.

He knocked and popped in. While he was there I had a quick look around the shop. It was very comfortable without being exactly Fortnum and Mason. There was a thickish carpet from wall to wall and the paintwork was all modern and bright.

On the walls were mock picture frames with various models of machines stuck in them at odd angles so that they looked like 3-D pictures. Over to one side of the shop was a display of their cabinet models and along the other wall were four cubicles with velvet curtains which could be drawn for privacy. Three of the cubicles were empty but the curtain of the fourth was pulled across and I could hear a man's voice instructing a woman on how to use the machine. From what I could hear she was making a terrible cock-up of it. I couldn't be sure but I think she'd just sewn his tie to her dress.

It was certainly a nice-looking shop.

Draper advanced on me as though he was greeting the Duke of Edinburgh and walked me into the office. Sitting behind a modest desk was Jimmy Sands.

Now he was a different proposition. There was nothing playboy about Sands. He was small and very stocky and his eyes took in every detail from the cut of my hair to the polish on my shoes in one lazy, lightning-fast glance. His smile was friendly enough but reserved and I got the distinct feeling that he never smiled at anyone unless he really wanted to. He was fairly young, like Draper, but his build and manner made him seem much older.

He stood up and gave me a firm hand.

'I'm Jimmy Sands, Mr Tobin. Please sit down.'

As I dropped into a black leather chair, Draper said, 'I'll be back in a minute, Jim. I'll just lock up the shop,' and he left us.

Sands offered me a cigarette and for a moment I didn't know whether to take one. Was this a trick? Was he trying me out? Were people supposed to smoke at interviews? And then I thought of what Stanford had said about being natural and confident and I thought bugger it, if a fag was going to lose me the job, then it wasn't worth having in the first place. So I took it and he lit it for me with a gold Ronson. Then he lit one for himself.

'Jim Stanford tells me you're interested in selling for us,' he began. 'Have you sold anything before?'

I shook my head. 'No, I've always done clerical work.'

'And you want to change?'

He grinned as if he knew what it meant to do clerical work and want to change.

'Yes,' I said.

'What makes you think you can sell?' He asked it pleasantly enough but there was a lot going on in his eyes.

I cleared my throat and shifted in my chair. 'Well, the idea of selling appeals to me—the variety of the job, meeting people. I get on well with people normally so there's no reason why I shouldn't do the same thing while I'm persuading them to buy something. I suppose, in a way, everybody is selling something to somebody all the time, whether it's a sewing machine or a service of some kind—like clerical work.'

It was damned corny stuff but it was obviously the right thing to say. Sands nodded enthusiastically and smiled all over his face and I knew I was in.

'Perfectly true, Mr Tobin. That's exactly what we tell our salesmen. Sell yourself first and the machine comes a natural second—well, most of the time, anyway.'

He leaned back in his chair and seemed a lot less officious. He eyed me for a moment and then nodded.

'I'd like to give you a trial, Mr Tobin. You look well and talk well and I can't see any reason why you shouldn't do well.' He dropped his ash into the silver ashtray in front of him. 'All my boys do well because the ones who don't, don't stay.' He laughed. 'I don't wish that to sound threatening but if a man isn't selling he's no good to me and he's no good to himself, so we part company.'

He leaned forward again and put one elbow on the desk.

'Now, Stanford tells me you're leaving your present job this Saturday. Is that right?'

'Yes, that's right.'

'And he also tells me you haven't got a car yet.'

I shook my head. 'No, but he's trying to fix something with

your garage. They've got one coming in in about two weeks time that sounds promising.'

Sands nodded. 'Good, that's splendid. That works out fine because I'd like you to spend a week in our service department and a week in training. We know that it benefits a salesman tremendously if he knows how to take a machine to pieces and put it together again. Then, if anything mechanical goes wrong while he's making a sale, he doesn't lose the sale because of it. There's nothing so face-saving and impressive as a salesman who can confidently fix a mishap on the spot.

'Then a week in training means that you'll be going out with an experienced man, probably with Jim Stanford, on actual home calls and also attending our sales meeting here in the shop on Monday morning. At the end of two weeks you should be ready to start on your own.'

That sounded pretty good to me. They obviously took a lot of trouble to get the new boys started well.

Sands went on to explain the system of selling just as Jim Stanford had done in the club and then he got on to the important part—the money.

'We pay commission only, as you probably know, but there are incentives. Firstly, we give you a good petrol allowance if you sell four machines a week and then, in addition to the five pounds per sale, you get an extra two pounds per sale if you sell ten or more a week. And for the first two weeks when you won't be earning at all, we'll advance you fifteen pounds a week against future earnings. That'll keep the wolf from the door. Does that sound fair?'

I told him it was fine and he stood up.

'Good. We'll just go out and tell Mr Draper that you're joining us and you can meet Mr O'Neill, our sales supervisor.'

We went back into the shop where Draper was just closing the door behind a departing customer. He slammed the bolts and came over to us.

Sands said, 'Allen, Mr Tobin would like to have a crack at selling for us. He'll be starting on Monday.'

Draper held out his hand and gave me the teeth again.

'Delighted! I'm sure you'll do very well and we'll see that you do. We want you to make lots of money—for you and us.' He laughed very heartily and slapped me on the shoulder.

Then, from the booth that had been occupied when I arrived, came a skinny little fellow with curly red hair. He was very nattily dressed in a dark blue suit and a polka-dotted bow tie and he moved quickly like a sparrow. His eyes were bird-like, too. They darted hither and thither in quick jerks as though the Gestapo were after him. Instinctively I didn't like him. He looked snide.

He came over to us and Sands introduced us. O'Neill gave me a disinterested hand and didn't look at me while he was saying how d'you do.

'Mr O'Neill is our sales supervisor,' said Draper. 'He's in charge of the salesmen, as it were. If you have any problems he'll sort them out for you.'

'That's right,' said O'Neill, in a thin Cockney voice, 'if you're not selling well, you just come to Tom O'Neill and we'll have you sorted out in no time. You may think you've got an insurmountable problem, but believe me, there's nothing left that I haven't run into and beaten in my time. There's no such thing as "can't" in my book, Tobin.'

Cockey little sod. Well, there he was. There just had to be a McFadden somewhere around. Well, frig him. He wasn't going to spoil things now. All the rest seemed so good.

'Right,' said Sands. 'We'll see you at nine o'clock on Monday morning.'

O'Neill wandered off without saying a word but Draper saw me to the door and smiled me off the premises which made me feel better.

On the way home my mind was buzzing with sewing machines. I liked Draper and Sands and I liked the atmosphere of the shop. O'Neill was going to be difficult, that was sticking out like a giraffe's John Henry, but at least I was prepared for him. He wasn't going to surprise me on Monday morning.

I found a telephone that hadn't been vandalized and called Jim Stanford to tell him the news, but he wasn't in. So I went to a little restaurant and had a quiet bite and then called him again. This time he was in and he said how pleased he was about me joining Ritebuy.

'Don't worry about O'Neill,' he said lightly. 'He's like our canary—all noise and droppings. If you were a little fellow with a face like his you'd probably be the same. Just grin at him, Russ, and pretend he's human and you'll be all right.'

I put the phone down feeling much happier about O'Neill and that meant I was happy about everything. Now I was really looking forward to Monday morning.

FIVE

Thursday and Friday crawled by like a fortnight, although in a funny way I rather enjoyed it. Now that I knew that the Ritebuy job was in the bag I could sit back and tantalize myself with my last couple of days at Wainwright's, like a kid who leaves the cherry off the cake until the last bite because he knows he can eat it any time he likes.

The whole atmosphere of the office had changed now. Mrs Reader was so polite it was painful and even McFadden nodded and grunted 'Good morning' in the corridor on Friday. Funny, isn't it, how nice people can be when they put their minds to it?

Gloria seemed a little bit strange. Oh, she kidded around as she'd always done but somehow her heart wasn't in it. She seemed depressed underneath the banter.

On Friday afternoon, my last day, I bought a cake, a great messy job with cream and jam in it and walnuts on top and we had it with our tea at half past three. They all said stupid things and made cracks about me and about McFadden and Wainwright's and about how frustrated Gloria was going to be unless they got a replacement as good-looking as me (they didn't know the half of it!) and then Mrs Reader of all people handed me a little parcel and said it was a farewell present from them all.

It was a Ronson gas lighter, a real beauty with a windguard and adjustable flame and it had my initials engraved on the side. I was really touched by it. I mumbled, 'Oh, you shouldn't have' and made a little speech which everybody laughed too heartily at and then there was a big embarrassed silence. I tried to break it by handing round cigarettes and lighting them with my new lighter but it wasn't very successful, and then, bless his moth-eaten sporran, in walked McFadden and saved the day. He yacked with Bob Fitch for long enough to settle us all back to work and the hiatus was over.

At five o'clock Bob Fitch and the two ladies said a final farewell and wished me the best of luck and then left for their buses.

'Coming?' I said to Gloria.

She gave me a hug and her hair smelt wonderful, fresh and

scented. I kissed her on the top of the head and put my arm round her and then suddenly I could feel her getting all hot and bothered.

She slipped her hands under my jacket and pressed me hard to her body.

'Oh, Russ,' she said softly, 'I wish you weren't leaving. This place is going to be awful without you.'

I must say she looked pretty miserable.

'Never mind,' I said. 'You're going to see lots of me in the future.'

She nodded but still looked miserable. I think this business with her husband was getting her down.

'Russ,' she said. 'Take me out tonight. Could you?'

I was a bit surprised about that.

'What about your husband? I thought he wasn't leaving until Sunday.'

She shook her head. 'We had another row last night. He packed his things and left this morning. He won't come back now.'

So that's why she was so miserable, what with me leaving and her husband leaving and the week-end in an empty flat coming up.

I hugged her and smiled down at her. 'Of course I'll take you out. Where would you like to go?'

Her eyes sparkled again and I could tell she was feeling much better. 'Anywhere, it doesn't matter.'

'How about a dance?'

'Yes! You know, I haven't been to a dance in two years.'

'Neither have I,' I said. 'I'll probably spend more time on your toes than my own.'

She went to get her coat and I helped her on with it.

'I'm right out of practice, too,' she said, 'but it doesn't matter, does it?'

She was really excited about it now.

'Not a bit. What time shall I pick you up?'

We went out into the corridor arm in arm.

'As early as you like. Give me time for a bath and a change, and I'm all yours.'

'Promise?'

She squeezed my arm and winked a very naughty wink.

'What do you think?'

Gloria's flat was on the ground floor in a small block of ten.

The place looked neat and clean and had a nice strip of lawn in front with a few empty flower beds.

On the door of number two was a small card in a thin metal frame and it said: 'Mr and Mrs C. Thomas' and I thought that's a lie for a start 'cos Charlie doesn't live here any more.

I pressed the bell push and heard tinkly chimes in the hall and in a few seconds the door opened and there was Gloria. To say that she looked like Faberge's top model would have been a wicked understatement. She looked fabulous. Her brown hair was shining like a Derby winner and her breasts were pushing a white Grecian-line dress into the most delectable shapes. She gave me a big snow-white grin and her eyes twinkled like a couple of sparklers.

'Come in, I'm nearly ready,' she said.

As I stepped into the hall I got a funny feeling, as though I was intruding, even though her husband had gone and good riddance. She took me into the lounge and said, 'Sit down, I'll be two minutes.'

When she'd gone into the bedroom the feeling came on stronger. I sat in an armchair and wondered if it had been his chair. I looked around the room and saw little things that said a man had lived there until a moment ago—a pair of mother-of-pearl cuff-links in a glass dish on the sideboard, an empty miniature cigar packet waiting to be thrown out. There was a T.V. set looking at me from the corner and I suddenly saw him get out of the other armchair and switch it on and then flop back to look at the *Radio Times* while the set warmed up.

His ghost was still warm in the room and it made me fidget.

Gloria came back in with her coat and I got up and helped her on with it. She smiled at me with her shining eyes and I was very glad that was all she did because I couldn't have even kissed her with his smell so strong in the room.

The dance wasn't such a good idea after all because in the two years since we'd last been to places like the Palais things had changed too much. The place was full of beatniks; long-haired nasties who looked rough enough to knife you if you so much as bumped into them—and that was only the girls!

I could see Gloria was disappointed and it was no atmosphere to romance in so we got out quickly. We had a walk through town and I showed her the Ritebuy shop, which she

46

liked very much, and then we found a quiet pub down a little side-street.

I got her a gin and bitter lemon and I had a beer and we sat at a corner table and lit cigarettes with my new lighter.

'We must be getting old,' I said, laughing.

She smiled and nodded. 'Two years makes a big difference. I've never heard of half the dances they do nowadays.'

'They make them up just before they go in,' I said, and then laughed. 'Listen to us! We sound like a couple of eighty-year-olds criticizing the youth of today.'

She laughed. 'And I felt like one with that bunch.' She opened her coat and looked down at her dress. 'I've never felt so over-dressed in all my life.'

'You were a knock-out,' I said, and meant it. 'The fellows couldn't take their eyes off you. I was jealous.'

She put her hand on mine. 'You are sweet, Russ.'

There was that look in her eye again and I felt my breathing go all potty as if someone had sprayed the room with nerve gas. I went quite dizzy and had to take a drink of beer to get my eyes right. She knew what she was doing, too, and then suddenly the same thing was happening to her. I could see her breasts begin to heave and a strange glassy look came into her eyes. When she spoke her voice was as strangled as mine.

'Let's go home, Russ. Now!'

For a moment I thought about her flat and the ghosts that were still living there, but now they didn't seem to matter. There was one overwhelming need in both of us which was far too physical to be frustrated by anything intangible.

I nodded and we got out quickly. We couldn't wait for a bus so I flagged a taxi and decided to regret the cost later on. It was nice, in the cab. She snuggled up for a little while as if to thank me for doing things properly, then, after she'd warmed up a bit, she lifted her face and kissed me very softly. Her mouth was warm and sweet and softer than I'd ever known a girl's mouth before, and then I knew what it was like to be kissed by an experienced woman who was bursting at the seams with want. My hand strayed to her knee and I felt her open up for me. I let my hand ride slowly up until I felt once again the hot flesh of her thigh, and then, by a strange mutual feeling, we both wanted me to stop. She closed her thighs and trapped my hand there until the taxi stopped.

She closed the front door and kissed me a little peck on the nose, then, taking my hand, she led me into the bedroom and

47

to the big double bed with the white candlewick bedspread. She slipped off her coat, then came to me and helped me off with mine. From then on there was a beautiful silence between us and everything was slow and leisurely and comfortable. It had never been like this before. There had always been, for me, embarrassment, hurry, furtiveness, and now, with Gloria, it seemed the most natural and beautiful thing in the world to strip naked before each other and make love.

When I finally left her it was Sunday evening. At the door she wrapped her arms around me and pressed me to her. Her voice was still sleepy from the afternoon.

'Russ ... that was wonderful. I never thought it could be so good.' She shook back her hair and looked up at me. 'I want to see you again ... anytime, but only when you're ready to come round. There's no obligation ... no ties. Remember that, no ties.'

I kissed her gently and then, in the outside hall, turned to look at her once more. She looked good, relaxed and happy and brim-full of satisfaction. I blew her a kiss and went down the road for a bus, feeling so damned conceited I couldn't stand myself.

SIX

It wouldn't have been natural not to be nervous on Monday morning, so I was. But then, as I walked into Ritebuy, I saw Jim Stanford and his familiar face quietened the butterflies considerably.

'Welcome to the club,' he said, all bright and breezy, just to make me feel at home. 'We'll go through to the Bored Room—B.O.R.E.D.—that's where we all get bored by O'Neill telling us how he used to sell fifteen thousand machines a week when he was a lad. It happens every Monday morning.'

He opened a door next to Jimmy Sands' office and we went in. It was a fairly large room with folding metal chairs set out in two rows of six and it had a raised platform at the far end with a table on it. There were twelve salesmen standing around near the chairs, chatting and laughing and smoking like steam trains leaving Lime Street station, and on the dais Allen Draper and O'Neill were talking.

Jim Stanford took me over to the group and introduced me. They all seemed nice fellows. Then Draper finished talking to O'Neill and said in a loud voice, 'Right! Good morning, gentlemen. Pray be seated.'

He was obviously in a good mood but he had bags under his eyes as big as kitbags and seemed to be making a big effort to stay awake. I didn't know how Draper spent his week-ends but the bags hadn't come from knitting in poor light, I'd have put money on that.

'Firstly,' he said, 'I'd like to welcome a new member to our midst—Mr Russell Tobin. Stand up, Russ!'

I got up a bit self-consciously and bowed to the fellows who were giving me a clap and then sat down again.

'And I'd like to explain for Russ's benefit that we meet here every Monday morning for our weekly pep pill—a little psychological shot in the arm to start the week off with a bang. Now...' he consulted a piece of paper, '... last week was pretty fair, gentlemen. Three of you did more than ten machines and you were all over five. Not the best week we've had, but not bad at all. Now, I think with Russ here today, this might be a good time to have another of our mock sales demonstrations with Mr O'Neill acting the part of the difficult housewife and one of you more experienced men making the pitch. Jim Stanford, how would you like to have a go?'

Jim muttered something choicely obscene under his breath but said, 'All right, Allen.'

'Good boy,' said Draper.

Jim went forward to the platform and O'Neill took his place in the chair by the table.

Jim knocked on the table as though it was a front door.

'Good morning, madam. My name is Stanford. I'm from Ritebuy Sewing Machines. We received a coupon from you asking for a demonstration on the famous Ritebuy Minor and I've brought it round for you.'

'Ah, yes,' said O'Neill. 'Do come in. Here, you can put it on that little coffee table.'

'Er ... if you don't mind, madam, I'd prefer that larger dining table ...'

'Why?' snapped O'Neill. 'This coffee table is big enough, isn't it?'

Jim shook his head. 'Not really, madam. You see, you will be sewing on this machine in a moment and I'm sure you'd prefer a bit more elbow room.'

'Yes, all right,' said O'Neill grudgingly.

Then Allen Draper interrupted them. 'Now, take a note of this, Russ. It is essential to give yourself enough room to work in—you'll see why in a minute. But never, never cramp yourself if you can help it.'

He nodded to Stanford who started unpacking the Ritebuy Minor. While he was taking the lid off and plugging the machine in, he was saying, 'Do you have any children, madam?'

'Oh, yes, one little boy. He's a terror.'

'And do you have a sewing machine already?'

'Yes,' said O'Neill. 'I've got an old treadle. We've had it for years. It used to be my mother's.'

He put on a high-pitched female voice and we all felt obliged to laugh at him.

'Good,' laughed Stanford. 'Now, here we are, Mrs O'Neill. This is the Ritebuy Minor you saw advertised ...'

O'Neill sniffed. 'Bit small, isn't it?'

'Ah, this is a three-quarter head machine—what we call a "compact" in the trade. It may look small but believe me it's very good value for the money. The benefit is in the lack of

50

weight, you see. It really is remarkably light.'

O'Neill sniffed again. 'Yes, go on,' he said dubiously.

'Right! Well, to start with, you'll see that the machine is enclosed in this very attractive carrying case, making it very portable. Then there is a first class motor and combined sewing light—here, and on the floor, the very latest foot control to operate it. Here is the stitch control lever and this lever here is to raise and lower the sewing foot. Now, I'll take this piece of demonstration cloth and show you how it sews. It really is simplicity itself.'

Stanford ran over the thin strip of cloth several times in different stitch lengths and then handed the cloth to O'Neill who pretended to examine it thoroughly.

'There!' said Stanford. 'Perfect sewing from a remarkably inexpensive machine. As you know, madam, the price is a very low four pounds nineteen and sixpence and might I ask how you were intending to pay for it—by cash or cheque? A cheque is perfectly acceptable, of course.'

'Er . . . cheque, yes,' said O'Neill. 'But . . .'

'Fine,' interrupted Stanford. 'I'll just write you out a receipt . . .'

'Good!' said Draper, stepping forward again. 'Fine, Jim. Now, Russ, that is the first part of the sale accomplished and Jim did it very well. He was pleasant but firm all the way through. He controlled the sale. At no time was Mrs O'Neill aware that she was being pressured but there was just that soupcon of guidance on Jim's part. He fought for—and got—his big table; he found out that she has a family and owns an old sewing machine, which is very important as you will see in a moment. He explained the machine concisely and without fuss and did a neat, quick demonstration of sewing. Then, at the end, he quickly came on to the subject of payment and had Mrs O'Neill committing herself with regard to method of payment, i.e. by cheque. In other words he was asking for the money in the nicest possible way. And don't forget, Russ—and all you other gentlemen, too—that more sales have been lost through the salesman's inability to close—that is, to ask for the money—than through any other reason. You must ASK FOR THE MONEY!'

He turned and grinned at Jim Stanford. 'Right, Jim, you've just made a sale. Go on from there.'

Stanford handed a fictitious receipt to Mrs O'Neill and said, 'Right, thank you very much indeed, Mrs O'Neill. I'm sure this machine will ... Oh, by the way, did you happen to hear our advert on commercial radio last night?'

O'Neill shook his head and looked offended. 'No, I'm afraid I don't listen to that rubbish.'

Stanford laughed. 'Well, I agree, some of the programmes are rubbish but there was certainly nothing rubbishy about our Special Offer. Just a moment, I'm sure this will interest you very much ...'

Allen Draper interrupted again. 'Now, at this point, Russ, Jim is going back to the car and is bringing in the Major machine. Notice that he puts it next to the Minor which Mrs O'Neill has just bought. You see now why he insisted on a large table. Go ahead, Jim.'

Stanford plonked the heavier and more expensive-looking carrying case next to the Minor and immediately the difference in quality was obvious. Mrs O'Neill looked suitably intrigued. Then Stanford whipped off the cover to reveal a big, black, gleaming beauty, a Rolls-Royce beside a roller skate.

'Oh, my word,' gushed O'Neill. 'What a beautiful machine! But of course I could never afford one like that in a million years.'

Stanford looked puzzled. 'But you wouldn't want to buy this one, madam. You've just bought this, haven't you?'

Stanford picked up the Minor as if it was a tin of corned beef and plonked it down again.

'And, for the money,' he went on, reserve creeping into his voice, 'that's a very good little machine. No, I'm not here to sell you this beauty, madam, but I do get paid a commission to demonstrate it to you, so that you will tell your friends and relatives about it. Now, firstly, you will notice the difference in size between this and the one you've just bought. This is a full-size machine, of course ...'

Well, now, I'm not going to bore you by going through the entire demonstration which took the best part of fifteen minutes, but I will tell you that Jim Stanford did a marvellous job on Mrs O'Neill. He demonstrated the pleater, the quilter, the hemmer, the button-holer with great flair and with each point that he made in the Major's favour, he never lost an opportunity to subtly knock the poor old Minor until Mrs O'Neill was going balmy with regret at having bought it. Then, at just the right moment, Jim pounced. He told her that he'd give her a wacking big trade-in price for her old machine (which he simply added on to the original price of the Major and then knocked it off again, so he got it for nothing!) and when he suggested that she could meet the monthly payments out of the child's allowance, Mrs O'Neill bit.

'Splendid!' said Allen Draper, jumping up. 'First class, Jim. A very good dem.' He turned to the rest of us. 'There you are, gentlemen, that's how to sell sewing machines. You'll meet objections, of course, that haven't been brought out here, but the thing is to try, try, TRY! all the time. Make up your minds before you knock on that front door that you are going to sell a machine to that customer and never admit defeat until you know you've given it everything you've got.'

He looked at his watch.

'Fine, gentlemen. We'll break now and you can collect your leads for today. Good selling! Er . . . Russ!'

He came down off the platform and said to me, 'Just have a seat for a minute. I'll see these lads off and then I'll be right with you.'

He left the room with the others and for a moment I was alone. So that's how it was done. Well, it didn't seem too difficult. I could sell them, I was certain.

My mind began to wander as I sat staring into the wall. I was knocking on the door of a grand house and a liveried footman bowed me into a vast golden hall. Down the sweeping staircase came a fabulous blonde in a see-through nightie. She floated across and we went into the library and I started the dem. Then she put her hand on mine and drew me towards the couch.

'Screw the machines, sweetie,' she whispered. 'I'll take six of the big ones but I want you first.'

'Cash or cheque?' I murmured.

'Show me how your button-holer works,' she said, taking off the nightie.

'Well, Russ,' said Draper. 'What d'you think of it all up to now?'

'I thought it was very impressive,' I said. 'I'm dying to have a crack at it.'

'Good boy. Oh, one thing I forgot to tell you. Don't ever leave the Minor in the house as a sale—it costs us money. If you can't sell the Major then kill the sale entirely.'

'I understand.'

He took my arm. 'Now we'll go into the workshop and meet Charlie Kingly, the mechanic.' He led me out of the dem room and down a short passage. 'Don't be put off by Charlie,' he said laughing, 'he's just a natural moaner. He grumbles from nine until five. Anyway, you've only got him for a week.'

He pushed through a door and we went into the stockroom. Banked on both sides and reaching to the ceiling were wooden boxes containing sewing machines, carrying cases, foot-controls and sewing lights. Sewing machine carcasses were strewn about in a tidy heap. We stepped through this lot and went into the workshop. There was a long wooden bench with two vices, tool racks, shelves—and Charlie Kingly.

He stood all of five foot two and was as skinny as a twig. He was shuffling around the room as though he'd just lost a thousand quid and found sixpence and all the time muttering to himself as if he was putting curses on the poor dumb machines. He looked up sourly as we went in and then returned his venom to an old Singer trade-in.

'Charlie, this is Mr Russell Tobin, our new salesman,' said Draper. Charlie gave me a cursory nod and heaved a Major on to the bench with surprising ease. I was expecting his arm to fall off his body.

Draper winked at me and went on, 'Mr Tobin will be spending a week with you, Charlie, so show him the ropes, won't you?'

Charlie grunted and started removing the hinge screws that kept the machine in the case.

'Right then, I'll leave you in Charlie's very capable hands,' said Draper, laughing inwardly and making a gesture of helplessness. He went out, still grinning, and I stood there like a stuffed duck for the next three minutes while Charlie got the screws out.

'Right,' he said at last, with as much enthusiasm as a bloke about to be shot. 'This is the Major, the one you'll be selling. It's a round bobbin machine with removable race and drop-feed mechanism . . .'

In the next half hour he took all the removable pieces off the machine and made me put them back again; he showed me in slow motion how a stitch was formed; he explained the top and bottom tensions; he showed me how to quieten a noisy machine, and he demonstrated the attachments. All of which was very interesting to me because I am quite mechanically minded and I was beginning to like the feel of the machines.

Charlie was surprisingly patient and even cracked a smile now and again and I was beginning to feel that his brusqueness was only a big act and that underneath it he was a nice little fellow. Over a cup of tea at eleven o'clock we sat on a couple of stools by the bench and he got quite chatty.

'Interesting things, machines,' he said into his tea. 'They're ... constructive, know what I mean?' He took a gulp and a drag from his home-made cigarette which smelt sweet and pungent and brought back memories of a tiny cigarette shop that my father had used when I was a kid.

'It's nice to find something totally constructive in a world hell-bent on destruction,' he said, almost to himself. He tapped the Major with his finger and then wiped away the print which he'd left on the oily surface.

'This is not a bad one. There are much better ones, of course ... the Elna, Necchi and so on. But you can sell the Major with a clear conscience.'

'What about the Minor?' I asked him.

He curled his lip and shrugged. 'It's worth the fiver—just about.'

We yacked about machines for a bit and then I asked him what he did all day. He waved his cigarette in several directions around the room. 'Too damned much!' he said heatedly. 'I've got to unpack the Majors and the Minors and stick motors and lights on them and then put them in carrying cases—and make sure they're sewing properly. You blokes would never sell one unless they were sewing properly! And then there's the trade-ins and the regular servicing on top of all that...'

'Servicing in the home, you mean, Charlie?'

He shook his head. ''Ere, give us a chance, mate. I couldn't very well do house calls and all this too, now could I? No, I've got a young lad—Vince, his name is—he does the house calls but very often he brings a machine in 'cos he can't fix it out there. You'll be meeting him at lunchtime—and serves you right!'

He raised his eyes to the ceiling in a gesture of hopelessness.

'What's he like?' I laughed.

He shook his head and decapitated his cigarette on to the floor, stowing the butt away for later.

'Love's young dream,' he said, grinning. 'He thinks he's Mick Jagger and that John Lennon all in one go and really he doesn't know what day of the week it is. If you're in that service van of his you can't hear yourself think. He's got his transistor going full blast from nine till five.'

I did meet Vince at lunchtime. He came in blowing on his blue hands and cursing the cold and cursing his 'bloody old clapped out van that had no heater and more holes in it than his ma's colander'.

He was very tall, had flaming red hair and was built like a moulting pipe-cleaner. Mick Jagger and John Lennon would have been insulted.

He stopped cursing long enough to shake my hand and give me a nice enough grin and then he was straight back at it.

'Cruddy old wreck ... the pistons are rattling around like four dried peas in a tin,' he said, rubbing life back into his bony digits. 'When are those two mean buggers going to get me something decent to drive?'

He flung a skinny arm in the direction of Sands and Draper and caught his hand on the stack of Minors. He let out a yowl of agony and went dancing round the workshop with his throbbing extremity stuck between his thighs for warmth and comfort. He looked like a kangaroo mother trying to get a dozen hungry fleas out of her pouch.

At that moment Allen Draper came through the door and stood rooted, watching Vince's performance with a huge grin.

'What on earth's the matter with you?' he laughed.

Vince flung out his arm, more carefully this time, in the direction of the offending vehicle.

'It's that van, sir! It's falling to pieces. I don't think it'll last another day.'

Draper nodded noncommittally. 'Yes, so you've said before, Vince, and we've promised you another one in due time. Just have a little patience and we'll get you a station waggon.'

He looked at me and winked. 'Well, how are you getting on, Russ?' He transferred his smile to Charlie. 'Think he'll do, Charlie?'

Charlie nodded. 'He's a natural, sir. He's got a feeling for them.'

'Splendid,' he said. 'Not that I doubted it for a moment. 'Well, now, I think this afternoon you might go out with Vince and do some house calls. It'll give you a chance to meet some of our customers and get used to knocking on doors.' He gave Charlie and me a wink. 'And, of course, to see how efficiently Vince deals with the problems.'

Vince let out a big derisive laugh that didn't fool anybody.

'Yeh, if I don't get frost-bite on the way,' he laughed. 'Mr Tobin had better put his long-johns on if he's coming in that crate.'

'He'll be all right,' said Draper smoothly. 'He'll have music to smooth his troubled breast.'

'It wasn't his breast I was thinking of,' said Vince.

Draper turned to leave. 'See you when you get back,' he said to me over his shoulder.

Vince hadn't been exaggerating all that much. We were caught in a crossfire of icy blasts that shot in from the floor, dashboard, windows and rear doors. Even the windshield seemed to be leaking. And the knock in the engine really was like four starving woodpeckers going berserk in Epping Forest.

'The clutch slips, too,' Vince shouted. Well, he had to shout to compete with the four billion decibels of screech and jangle coming from his transistor.

'Could we have it a little lower?' I shouted back.

'Eh?'

I pointed to the chromium-plated thunder machine and pulled an agonized face. He looked a little puzzled that I should think it too loud and reluctantly turned it down to mere deafening level.

'Where's the first call?' I asked him.

He reached for a clip-board and did some suicidal one-hand driving with two fingers without losing the beat of the drums with the other three.

'Scotland Road,' he read.

I shuddered as he steered the van between a double-decker bus and an oncoming oil tanker without apparently looking up from the board. Then he had two panic-stricken pedestrians scuttling for their lives from a pedestrian crossing and skidded to within a thickness of chrome from the back of a Bentley at some traffic lights.

'Been driving long?' I asked.

'Oh, yes ...' he said, sounding like Jack Brabham. 'Six months.'

'You drive very well, Vince,' I said. 'You haven't killed a soul since we started out.'

He grinned and shook his head. 'Never do on Mondays. Starts the week off on the wrong foot.'

The lights changed and I was thrown into the back of the seat as the woodpeckers started their racket and the seventeen different sub-zero hurricanes swept in again. A year later, it seemed, we pulled up outside a filthy, two-storeyed slum tenement just off Scotland Road.

The dirty, narrow street rose sharply from the main road and when we parked, Vince had to yank the wheels hard over to the curb to dissuade the van from rolling back and disappearing down the Mersey Tunnel. The moment we stopped, about four thousand snotty-nosed kids swarmed out of the tenement and surrounded the van. God, they were a sight—all dirty and sniffing and not one of them had a decent coat on. Some were chewing jam butties and had more jam on their faces than on the bread, but, surprisingly, they all looked happy enough.

Vince stepped out and locked the van.

'Merely a gesture,' he muttered cynically. 'These little robbers could have the engine out in seven seconds if they put their minds to it. Here, you kids,' he shouted, 'clear off, now, and leave this bleedin' van alone. I don't want "I love Alik Doglus Hewm" on it when I get back!'

We pushed our way through the scruffy throng and walked up two flights of iron stairs to an iron verandah. From this height I could see right across the neighbourhood and a right depressing sight it was, too. Acres and acres of tight-packed houses and tenements; line after line of grey slate roofs running up the hill to the gigantic Catholic church which towered over everything like an episcopal Rock of Gibraltar. It looked solid, gaunt and immovable and seemed to be about to pat the little houses on the head and reassure them that things would improve soon. Grey washing hung in squalid backyards and babies cried in second-hand prams.

Down below us the kids were writing 'I love George Brown' in the dirt of Vince's van and one little shrimp in a red jersey was trying to wrench the sidelights off.

Vince leaned over the railing and shouted, 'Leave that alone, you kids!'

'Fuck off,' said a sweet little voice.

Vince shrugged at me and knocked on number seventy-two.

The door was opened by an apparition in hair curlers and a dirty apron with custard all down the front. At least I hoped it was custard. She had a baby in one arm and a fag-end stuck in her mouth.

'Yes?' she said, dropping ash on top of the custard.

'Ritebuy Sewing Machines, madam,' said Vince, screwing up his nose. The smell was powerful. It drifted out of the door like a thick mist floating over a stagnant bog and seemed heavy

58

enough to fall over the balcony with a crash.

'Oh, yes ... and about time,' she said, giving me a suspicious look through the fag smoke. She coughed a couple of good ones and stood aside to let us in.

We walked down the thick brown hallway and I began to feel ill. I don't think I'll ever get rid of that smell. It hit me in the face like a rotten apple and saturated my skin, hair and clothes just as physically as if I'd stepped under a shower of bad beer.

The living room was murky, lit only by what grey daylight had had nerve enough to penetrate the dirty window, but it was light enough to show the brown floral wallpaper and matching lino (*circa* 1906), the cheap, torn furniture and the old lady lying on a divan in the corner. She must have been three hundred years old. Her hair, what was left, was pulled sharply back into a bun, emphasizing the toothless, sucked-in face that was as wrinkled as an ugly fruit.

''ello, boys!' she croaked. ''ave they cum to fix the telly, Prucilla?'

Prucilla!

'No, the sewing machine, Gran. 'Ere, lad, there it is, over there.'

She nodded her fag into a dark corner and Vince went fumbling for the machine.

'What seems to be the trouble?' he asked politely.

'Won't sew.'

'Oh.'

Vince heaved the Major on to a table which seemed incapable of bearing its weight. It staggered a bit and splayed its legs like a giraffe getting down for a drink but it held.

''Ow about a light, missus?' said Vince.

Prucilla clicked on a miserable single bulb which was encased in a green fly-blown shade high in the ceiling and I wished she hadn't. The place was disgusting. There were soggy, half-chewed crusts on the table and a liberal sprinkling of jam on the lino. In the fireplace was the baby's potty which hadn't been emptied since last week and a bundle of dirty nappies were lying by it. I felt sick.

Vince looked up from the machine and pulled his nose at me in disgust and then gingerly took the cover off the machine. As he did so a fat black cockroach ran out and high-dived off the table on to the lino and scuttled across to the fireplace. Neither Prucilla nor Grannie seemed to notice.

59

'Want a chair?' Prucilla asked him.

Vince looked at the chair and saw the jam on the seat and shook his head.

'No thanks, we won't be a minute.'

He bent down to look at the machine and then I saw him get happy. He looked up and gave me a big wink.

'Oh, I see wot's the matter, missus. You've put the needle in sideways.'

He quickly unscrewed the needle grip and corrected the needle. Then, threading it, he tested it on a piece of dem cloth. I could hear him breath a sigh of relief when it sewed well. He whipped the lid back on the machine and stowed it back in the corner.

'No charge, missus. Good day!'

He was off like a shot with me right behind him.

'Won't you stop for a cup of tea?' asked Prucilla.

'Not right now, missus, thank you. We've got a lot of calls this afternoon. Tarra, Grannie!'

The old lady shouted, 'Tarra, son!' as we ran down the hall and then down the stairs.

Vince scattered the kids who had added 'All Tories are scabby pigs' and 'Mary luvs Doris—dirty bitch' to their other comment, and we got in the van.

We both breathed in big, deep breaths of fresh air as Vince started the engine and backed the van down to Scotland Road.

'Dirty pigs,' he said vehemently. 'There's no need for it, is there? Nobody's that poor any more. You can buy a bar of carbolic and a bottle of disinfectant for a couple of bob.' He looked back at the sad, grey street as we turned the corner. 'Whole bleeding lot wants blowing up.'

I nodded. 'I expect it will be soon. They're clearing all these slums now.'

'Huh!' he went. 'Won't make any difference. Put Prucilla and Grannie in a new flat and in a year it'll look just like that one. They wouldn't feel at home without the cockroaches and the stink.'

'Are they all like that?' I asked.

He shook his head. 'Oh, no. They're all badly off for furniture, mind you, but most of them are a damn-sight cleaner than that. That's the worst I've ever been in.'

He sniffed at his coat sleeve and pulled a face.

'It's gone right in, you know. I'll have to get this cleaned.'

I sniffed at mine and agreed.

He drove with casual frenzy up past the museum and into London Road, leaving behind him a wake of cursing, honking, gesticulating drivers and pedestrians.

'Ah, shurrup!' was all he ever said to indicate that he was aware of the mayhem erupting behind him. 'Shouldn't be allowed behind a wheel, most of 'em.'

'Yes,' I said. 'Where to now?'

He was about to do the two-finger bit with the steering wheel again but I got to the clip-board before him.

'116, Mountwood Road, Childwall,' I said, feeling inside me an excitement at the name Childwall—Gloria's district.

'Ah, that's better,' said Vince. 'I could do with a spot of Childwall after that last midden.'

He lowered his window and filled the cab with an icy blast of fresh air and then closed it again.

'Ah, that's better,' he said, breathing in until I thought his buttons would explode. 'Nothing like a good chestful of ozone.' He dipped into his pocket and handed me the packet. ' 'Ere, let's 'ave a fag.'

SEVEN

All the week I worked in the service department and enjoyed it. Some days, if Charlie had too much on his plate, I'd stay in the shop with him, uncrating the machines, putting on motors and sewing lights, doing a lot of fairly simple jobs while he got on with the more technical one. Then, on other days, I'd maybe spend the morning with Charlie and go out with Vince in the afternoon.

Despite his diabolical driving, I started to look forward to the house calls because they were teaching me a lot about people, you know, showing me their funnyocities and giving me a fair old insight into what a salesman could expect.

One thing stuck out a mile, too, and that is that people are really very nice. Oh, they can be downright peculiar, I know, but generally speaking they're a pretty nice bunch. But, another thing also was very apparent, and that is that we're all a bunch of Jekyll and Hydes if the truth were known. The man (or woman) in the street is one thing—they behave in a certain, rational, expected way (unless they're nuts, in which case they're usually not in the street for very long!)—but in the privacy of his or her home he or she is quite another thing.

Take the case of Mrs Henderson.

Charlie and I were working in the shop on Thursday and it was getting close to lunch time when Allen Draper came through from the front and said that a Mrs Henderson was in the shop and wanted service on her machine right away. Well, by his tone of voice Mrs Henderson sounded very important.

Charlie said to me, 'Go and see what she wants, Russ. Put it on a service form and get Vince to see to it this afternoon.'

I followed Draper back to the showroom and standing there, looking like a duchess in a fur coat and fur hat, was an imperious old darling in her sixties. She didn't quite whip out her pince-nez and look me up and down but I had the feeling she ought to. She gave me a pleasant enough but reserved smile when Draper introduced me and I felt instinctively that I ought to bow or something.

'Mr Tobin will look after you, madam,' said Draper and after blinding her with a big smile he swept away towards the cubicles.

'You'd like someone to check your machine?' I said.

She smiled at me again. 'Yes, if you'd be so kind. I can't think what's gone wrong with it. There's a curious "clicky" noise underneath.'

I wrote down 'clicky noise underneath' on the service form and filled in her name and address.

'Would it be at all possible to come this afternoon?' she pleaded.

Well, when a woman like that asks you for a favour you fall over yourself to do it, don't you?

'We'll certainly do our best, madam. You'll be in this afternoon?'

'Yes, I never go out in the afternoons.'

'Then we shall be there,' I said grandly.

Vince flipped when I told him.

'Oh, for God's sake, look at this bleedin' bunch I've got already!'

He brandished a wad of service forms at me and put old Charlie's fag out with the draught.

I shrugged. 'Sorry, Vince, but she's pretty important.'

So he shrugged and said, 'O.K. What's another one. But we'll have to get to her last.'

We got out to the Henderson house about half past four. It was a creepy-looking place, made even creepier by the rain that was pitching out of heaven by the thousand tons and making everything sodden and miserable.

The house was huge and old and rambling and reminded me of those sad, old giants round by the cricket club. It stood in its own tiny grounds which were full of my unfavourite trees and shrubs—faded hydrangeas and sooty privets and laurels.

There was a short, mossy path from the front gate to some porch steps which looked terribly ill and infirm. We closed the gate and walked up it.

'Cheerful place,' said Vince.

I pushed at a saucer-sized bell push and tried to keep the rain from filling up my coat while somebody answered it.

'Can you hear something?' said Vince, cocking his ear.

All I could hear was the rain overflowing from a waterspout and smacking into the ground by the porch. I shook my head.

'Music,' he said.

I cocked my ear and it seemed to help. Very faintly I could

hear the twanging guitars and the moronic monotone of the current top of the hit parade.

I pressed the bell again—longer this time.

'She probably can't hear,' Vince offered. 'How about knocking on a window?'

We waited a couple of jiffies longer and then started a safari through the dripping bushes. We looked quickly into large, high-ceilinged rooms, scantily furnished with old brown and green and mahogany things. Then we came to the kitchen.

It was a cavernous place, as the kitchens of these big houses are, and the white, scrubbed-wood table in the centre of the green lino floor looked like a tiny desert island in a vast ocean. On the table was a portable radio, a bottle of orange squash, a bottle of gin about three-quarters full, and a little pink birthday cake with five unlit candles stuck in it. And dancing around the table, a glass of gin and orange in her outstretched hand, was Mrs Henderson. But she looked very different now. Her eyes were closed and there was a blissful, dreamy smile on her lips. Her other hand held the hem of her silk floral dress and she was doing a graceful old-fashioned waltz to the wang and jangle that was belting out of the radio.

On the floor by the hall door lay an Alsatian which must have been sixteen hundred years old and as deaf as a yo-yo. It lay stretched out with its massive moth-eaten head on its moth-eaten paws and every now and then it would flick up a lugubrious eyebrow, check that the old girl was still at it, and then let the weighty eyebrow down again with obvious exhaustion.

'She's pissed,' whispered Vince. 'What are we going to do?'

I shrugged and regretted it because the rain fell off my upturned collar and ran down my neck.

'We did promise,' I said.

I reached up and tapped gently on the window. Nothing happened. Mrs Henderson did a couple more circuits of the table and drank some gin.

I knocked hard this time and the dog opened one eye. Then it saw us and all hell let loose. It shot across the floor with a speed I wouldn't have thought possible and thrust its terrifying brown teeth at us in a savage snarl. Mrs Henderson nearly dropped her gin. For a moment she just stood there, getting us in focus and trying to remember my vaguely familiar face. Then she gave up. She cocked a quizzical eye at us and I yelled, 'SEWING MACHINE!' through the glass.

She flashed a look of annoyance at the radio and then it suddenly occurred to her to turn it down. When she'd done this she resumed the quizzical look.

I felt in my pocket and found a business card and held it to the window. The dog started spitting all over the window, trying to eat both the card and my hand and Mrs Henderson advanced on it like a myopic vicar trying to find the lesson for today. Then she shook her head and made a gesture of 'wait a minute' and went off across the kitchen to her handbag.

'Oh, Christ!' muttered Vince.

Meanwhile the dog was going berserk and I could feel the house vibrating from the power of its bark.

'Let's come back when she's sober,' said Vince. 'I don't like the look of that bleedin' dog.'

I'd just about decided to do just that when Mrs Henderson came back with her specs on. She peered at the card and you could tell that even now she could hardly read the thing. However, something must have registered because suddenly she threw up her hands and beamed at us and started shifting four tons of Alsatian from the back door.

Eventually she opened it and stood with one hand on the doorknob and the other hooked in old Snarly's collar.

'Oh, bless me, I'm so sorry, boys. Do come in. Never mind Gladys here, she won't harm you.' She laughed gaily. 'Ha ha! She's too old to bite anyone—just like her mistress.'

I wasn't so sure of that—about Gladys, I mean.

'Now, go on—shoo!' she said to the dog and pushed at it with her kneecap. It reluctantly shuffled back across the lino to the hall doorway and flopped down like a sack of cement. Once again it lowered its head to its paws and let go a moan like a fog horn on the Mersey.

'Now, you be a good girl,' Mrs Henderson ordered and the faithful old dog's eyes said, 'Get stuffed.'

'Now then—oh, you poor boys, you're soaking wet! Take your coats off and I'll hang them by the stove.'

We shucked off the soggy garments and while she was draping them over a couple of wooden chairs by the boiler, she said, 'Did you ring the front door bell? I'm very sorry if I didn't hear you but I was having a little party, you see, all by myself and the radio was going ... and Gladys here is too deaf to hear herself bark, poor thing ...'

Gladys was still trying to decide which of us to eat first and

65

was growling way down in her stomach like a ten-wheeler going through the Mersey Tunnel.

'Is it your birthday, missus?' asked Vince.

The old girl smiled shyly and pointed at a couple of chairs that were tucked under the table and started to pull another one out for herself, but Vince, joining in with the spirit of the occasion, rushed round the table to hold the chair for her. Gladys, completely misinterpreting this surprising piece of gallantry, was on her feet before you could say 'Elastoplast' and had sunk her few remaining fangs clean through Vince's trouser leg.

Vince let out a yowl of terror that even Gladys must have heard and started leaping around the kitchen, dragging the Alsatian with him.

Mrs Henderson was having a fit. She was shouting, 'Gladys, let go of the nice gentleman! He didn't want to hurt mamma. Gladys! Go and lie down!'

But Gladys was having more fun than she'd had conceiving her last litter and was having a whale of a time being hauled round the lino by hysterical Vince. Round and round they went for about three circuits and then the inevitable happened. Vince's trousers zipped apart just below the knee and while he went hurtling down the hallway, Gladys shot across the slippery lino and finished up with her bottom on the hot boiler. For a second nothing happened, Gladys just sat there looking a bit puzzled, and then the cold (or rather hot) facts of what was happening got through to her. With a 'YIP!' that they must have heard in Bootle, Gladys bolted across the kitchen floor, slammed into the hallway door, skidded on the spot like a demented egg-beater, and then shot down the hallway, flattening Vince who was just getting up.

We heard the poor animal thundering up the stairs and then dragging its scorched bottom through every bedroom in the house.

Vince got off the floor and came running back into the kitchen, bolting the door behind him.

'That bloody thing's mad!' he shouted.

He looked down at his leg which was bare from his knee to the top of his purple nylon sock.

'Oh, what a terrible thing to happen!' gasped Mrs Henderson. 'Oh, you poor boy! Here, sit down ... let's all sit down and have a drink. I'm sure we all need one after that.'

Clutching her breast in anguish she went to a cupboard and

brought back two glasses.

'Oh, I've never known Gladys to behave like that before. Really, she's usually the most docile creature and she's seventeen years old, you know—I've had her since she was a puppy. And never, never has she attacked anybody before.'

She poured out three handsome slugs of gin and snicked in a soupçon of orange to colour it.

'There,' she said, pushing the glasses to us, 'drink that. I'm sure you'll feel better.'

We all took a good gulp and I could feel the near-neat alcohol cauterizing my breast-bone as it tumbled down; then, as it reached my lower ribs, it tripped off a minor power-station that started pumping a warm, cosy flush right through my body and up into my hair. I felt like floating off the chair and doing a few aerobatics around the ceiling.

I looked at Vince and I could see the same thing was happening to him. He'd turned a light puce. Mrs Henderson had already finished half her drink and just looked happy.

'Now, isn't that better?' she asked with a big smile.

'Much,' said Vince.

'This really is very good gin,' she said, reaching for the bottle. 'It's special gin, you know. I think it's a hundred and twenty proof or something. My son gets it from abroad. He's in the Merchant Navy.'

'Really,' said Vince politely. 'Yes, it is.'

'It is what?' asked Mrs Henderson, topping up her glass.

'Very good gin,' said Vince.

She took this as a request for more so she poured him another slug.

'Oh, no, no,' Vince protested, after she'd poured it.

'Oh, go on with you,' she smiled. 'You boys must have a drink with me on my birthday. It is my birthday, you know, and I've baked myself a little cake. Do you like it?'

She pulled the sad little cake across to her and I could see that written in shaky icing on the top was 'Happy Birthday, Henrietta'.

'Do you think that's silly . . . me making a cake for myself?'

I shook my head which now seemed to belong to somebody else. 'Not at all. I think it's very nice.'

She sighed and took another gulp.

'I'm afraid we tend to do silly little things when we get older . . . especially if we live alone. There's too much time to think, you see, boys . . .' She brightened suddenly. 'Oh, you're both too young to understand—and I'm very, very glad you are—but it's true.' She laughed. 'You'd think I was mad if you heard the way I talk to myself. I do, you know. I talk to myself all the time. Well, it's no good talking to Gladys any more because she can't hear a thing ... so I talk to myself and sing and dance around here all by myself...'

'Don't you have any friends?' I asked.

She emptied her glass and shook her head.

'No ... not really. I've got a sister who comes over from Manchester once a month but she's as deaf as Gladys. It's really quite a strain talking to her. She's got one of those deaf-aid things but she's always letting her batteries run down. Every time she comes here she seems to have a dud battery. I'm always telling her to carry a spare but she says they won't keep in her handbag.'

'How about neighbours?' I said.

She shook her head again and leaned forward to avoid being overheard.

'Don't like them.' She gestured over her left shoulder. 'These people are terribly common. You wouldn't believe the way they live. It wouldn't surprise me at all if they kept pigs in the bedroom. And that lot'—she stabbed a thumb at the wall behind Vince's back—'they're Arabs or somesuch. You should smell their cooking! Is it Arabs that eat sheep's eyeballs?'

'Yes, I believe it is,' Vince said knowledgeably, swaying in his chair.

'Well, that's exactly what it smells like. Boiled eyeballs!'

My stomach did a quick flip, so I took another gulp to pacify it. I was beginning to feel handsome.

'Oh, you're nearly out,' said Mrs Henderson and poured me another small quadruple.

'Tell me!' she said suddenly. 'How on earth do you young people remember all the new dances these days? I was watching television last night and I tried several of them but they defeat me, I'm afraid. What do you call them nowadays?'

Vince brightened—this was his territory. He'd been telling me on the rounds what a fiend he was for dancing. Three nights a week he was down at some club or other wearing his boots out.

'Well,' he said with casual grandeur, 'there's the Nutmeg and the Shuffle and the Fly Swat...'

'Oh, good gracious!' laughed Mrs Henderson. 'What names you think up. How on earth do you do all those?'

'I'll just show you!' said Vince, sounding like Gene Kelly about to show off to Cyd Charise.

He staggered out of his chair and fell over it.

'Let's have the table out of the way,' he laughed, picking himself up.

I grabbed one end and he took the other and we rushed it to the side of the kitchen. Then he turned on the radio and twiddled the dial until he got some hit parade rubbish.

'Ah, that's the Chicken Gizzard!' he announced and went into a tricky gyration, with his feet wobbling around all over the place and his arms flapping like a castrated cockerel.

'Come on, ma . . . join in!' he panted.

Mrs Henderson lined up in front of him and started doing the same thing and, by golly, she wasn't half bad. In about ten seconds she'd got it off pat and started doing a solo around the room, laughing her head off and thoroughly enjoying herself.

Just to show there was no ill feeling I started clapping out the beat and giving her some encouragement and we made a heck of a noise until the music finished.

Old Ma was puffed to beat the band but she was having a whale of a time.

'Oh . . .', she gasped, 'oh . . . that was very nice. Here, what's this one?'

Vince listened to the new row that was starting up. 'Ah, this is "Stuff And No Nonsense" by Imbie Seal and the Idiots,' he said confidently. 'It's a Sparrow's Ankle.'

'A what?'

'A Sparrow's Ankle. You pretend you're a sparrow, see, and you hop around as though you've got a sore leg . . .'

Mrs H. let out a whoop of laughter and started copying Vince who was clattering around the oilcloth and hopping first on one foot and then on the other and whistling like he was in pain.

To tell you the truth I'd never heard of a Sparrow's Ankle and, between you and me, I don't think Vince had either. He was just making the whole flaming thing up to give the old girl a laugh. And laugh she did. She was in tears.

And Gladys was back again. She was barking like blazes outside in the hall and scratching great cobs of varnish off the door.

'Don't let that dog in, for Pete's sake!' shouted Vince. 'He'll tear me legs off if he sees me dancing with you!'

'Go away, Gladys!' shouted the old girl. 'Stop that noise this instant!'

The dog took no notice, of course.

The tune ended and we all collapsed around the table again and Mrs H. poured us all another drink. We were so boozed by now that it just tasted like orange juice.

'Here's to you, Ma!' said Vince, raising his glass. 'A very Happy Birthday. Russ ... how about ... Happy Birthday to you ... Happy Birthday to yooouuu ... Happy Biiiirthday, Henriettaaaa ... Happy Birthday to yooooouuu.'

When we'd finished singing (?), Mrs Henderson looked at us for a moment, first at Vince and then at me, just like we were two sons back from the war and then her eyes filled with tears and she started crying.

Vince looked at me and then reached out and patted her on the hand. 'Ah, come on now, Ma. Don't cry. I thought you were having a nice time?'

She nodded her head and sniffed into her little hanky. 'Oh, I am, boys ... that's what I'm crying for. It's ... it's been lovely. Here I was, all prepared to eat my cake with Gladys and it's turned out so much better ...'

'Let's have some now!' I said, trying to stop her crying. 'Can we have some, ma?'

She dabbed at her eyes and smiled. 'Oh, of course you can.' She blew her nose and got up and brought some plates and knives from the cupboard and when she got back Vince had lit the five candles.

'Oh,' she said, a bit embarrassed. 'It ... it was a bit silly putting candles on, wasn't it?'

'Nah!' protested Vince. 'What's a birthday cake without candles? Go on, blow them out, ma—and make a wish.'

The old girl closed her eyes and blew them out in one go and then she started slicing the cake.

'Why five candles, ma?' I said, joking with her. 'One for every seven years of your life?'

She threw back her head and laughed and I could tell she was pleased with my little bit of schmultz.

'Oh, bless you, if only that were true. How I'd love to be thirty-five again ...'

She handed us the cake and it tasted very good.

'It's been thirty years since I was thirty-five,' she said wistfully. She shook her head and a sad, nostalgic look came into her eyes. 'Those were good days ... so very good. My husband

and I were living in China then ... he was in the army ... a major...'

She took a sip of gin but did it absent-mindedly because she was thousands of miles away.

'It was a good life. We had a lovely home with servants and a beautiful garden full of glorious flowers. There was a lily pond with goldfish and a little ornamental bridge crossing it ... we had lots of parties in that garden...'

She looked up suddenly towards the window as if expecting to see the guests arriving but instead she saw the icy rain pitching at the window and she shivered.

'It was never like this,' she said, almost in a whisper. She looked around the kitchen with its ugly lino and cheap furniture and she shook her head. The poor old dear looked suddenly lost and very miserable.

'How about your son?' I asked. 'How often do you see him?'

She shrugged and smiled. 'Not very often, I'm afraid. Richard commands an oil tanker and it never docks in England. I only see him during his leave.'

Vince shook his head, disgusted with the situation. 'Haven't you got anyone else?'

'No, only my sister. My dear dear husband died five years ago...'

Then she suddenly brightened. 'Oh, come now, what are we being so miserable for? We were having such a lovely time. What's your name, young man?'

'Russ,' I said. 'This is Vince.'

'Vince,' she said. 'You find some more music and we'll have another dance.'

Vince was dying to look at his watch. 'I ... er ... think we'd better call Ritebuy and tell them we had a puncture or something.'

Mrs H. looked puzzled. 'Ritebuy...?'

'Yes, Ritebuy Sewing Machines. It's where we work.'

'Oh, Lord!' she gasped. 'Of course ... the machine! I'd quite forgotten why you came here. Oh, I do hope you won't get into trouble...'

'Nah,' said Vince with alcoholic indifference. 'That van's always breaking down. I'll just ring them and tell them I'm getting the puncture fixed and I'll take the van home tonight.'

'Well, if you're quite sure...' said Mrs Henderson.

She got up, gingerly opened the hall door and grabbed

Gladys by the scruff of the neck.

'I'll lock her in the front room,' she said over her shoulder. 'The telephone's in the hall, Vince.'

Well, I'll tell you, we had a ball. We murdered the bottle of gin and we danced around like three lunatics and then old Ma made us a wonderful supper of steak, eggs and chips and she even produced a bottle of wine from the pantry.

We didn't leave until nearly eleven o'clock and it would have done you good to see how happy she was. She made us promise to go round any time we felt like it and to pop in for a free meal if we were ever broke. And Vince and I decided on the way home that we really would go and see her again and give her a bit of a giggle—provided she locked that flamin' dog up first!

And there you are, you see—that's how different people can be behind their own front doors. She looked so grand and la-de-dah in the shop and all the time she was just a lonely old woman dying for a bit of fun. Doesn't do to make up your mind about people too quickly, does it? You can come a heck of a cropper sometimes. More often than not they're pretty nice when you get to know them.

EIGHT

Well, that was my first week at Ritebuy and chock-a-block full of edification it had been, too.

On the following Monday morning Jimmy Sands called me into his office and he was all smiles, which was a fair sign that he was pleased about something.

'Sit down, Russ,' he said, so I did. Then he offered me a cigarette which I took and lit and he did the same and we settled down like two prime ministers about to discuss the fate of nations.

'Well, how did you enjoy your first week with us?'

'Very much indeed, sir.'

'No problems?'

I shook my head. 'No, sir. Everything's fine.'

'Splendid,' he said and blew some smoke at a fly on his blotter. 'Charlie was very complimentary about your work. He tells me you work hard and handle the machines as if you'd been doing it all your life.'

'Very good of Charlie,' I said humbly.

'So I think we can progress to the next step. This week I want you to go around with Jim Stanford and watch how he sells. I've had a word with him and he's more than agreeable.'

'Very good of Jim,' I said.

'Any news of the car yet?'

I shook my head. 'No, not yet. I'll ask Jim again this morning, though. Perhaps he can call the garage.'

Sands nodded. 'Good. Well, you go on into the sales meeting now and carry on with Jim afterwards.'

Stanford was already in the meeting and he greeted me like a long-lost brother because I hadn't seen him since the previous Thursday.

'How did you do on the week?' I asked him.

He gave me a wink and looked very pleased with himself.

'Fifteen,' he said nonchalantly.

'Eh!'

'Not bad, hm?'

I laughed. 'No, not bad.'

'And you'll be doing that soon,' he said confidently. 'I'll give you a work-out this week and then you can get cracking.'

'Fine,' I said. 'Oh, any news about the car yet?'

'I'll give them a ring after the meeting. They should know something this week.'

Allen Draper came in then, looking cheerful but even more worn out than last Monday. Boy, he certainly knew how to spend his week-ends.

He took his familiar sleepy-eyed, mellow-minded stance on the platform and tried to sound enthralled about the week's sales figures which were very good. Every man had done eight machines or better. Jim was top with his fifteen and drew a special mention from Draper and a generous round of applause from the lads.

Instead of a mock dem this week, O'Neill gave us a lecture on general principles of selling and didn't miss a single opportunity to remind us of his own personal achievements. It got very boring very quickly despite his filthy stories (or because of them) and the lads started shifting in their seats and coughing. Finally he got the message and shut up.

When we dispersed Jim Stanford went straight to the telephone and called the garage. After he'd spoken for a few minutes he put the phone down and said, 'All is well. It should be in on Thursday. That was Bob Butler—it's his garage—and he said he'll go over it on Thursday and we can have a look at it on Friday morning.'

From that moment I started to get excited about the car. Old banger it may be but it was going to be my first car and that's something to get excited about. Three years I'd been waiting for one—ever since I'd passed my driving test—and now it was only a couple of days away. My imagination started ticking over at a steady gallop. No more standing in queues in the perishing rain. No more dashing for the last bus and spoiling a good party. And the girls! Well, you can cut a bit of a dash with a car, can't you? There's nothing so amateurish and unsophisticated as saying, 'I'll see you to the bus stop, darling' or 'Help me find my trousers, honey, I'll miss my last train.'

No, a car gives a fellow a terrific edge; really separates the men from the boys.

Stanford was sorting out his four leads for the day.

'Good ... good ... good ... mmm ...'

'Something wrong?' I said.

He shrugged. 'Can't always tell, Russ. This last one's in a rather posh area and they can either be very good or awful.'

'How come?'

He sniffed. 'Well, wealthy people can either be the most difficult to sell to—they're careful, you see, that's how they've accumulated their money—or they can be very easy because they've got it to spend. You can never tell but usually they're a bunch of tight-wads.'

We went out into the yard at the back of the building where his new Consul was parked.

'I've already loaded up,' he said, grinning. 'I try to beat the others to it, otherwise I'm stuck here half the morning getting machines off Charlie. That's a tip for you. And here's another—try and park over this side of the yard, away from the others, otherwise you might get jammed in and still spend half the morning here.'

'Thanks,' I said.

'Don't mention it.'

He drove out of the yard and headed through the town which was still suffocating with the morning rush.

'Selling is so much a state of mind, Russ,' he said unexpectedly. 'Your attitude sticks out a mile to the customer, you know. If you knock on a front door feeling defeated—you're sunk, even before you put a foot over the mat.'

He avoided a swerving taxi with a flick of his wrist and I waited for him to lean on his horn and yell out of the window.

'Bloody fool,' I said for him.

He smiled at me. 'That's one thing I try not to do, Russ—get all steamed up when I'm driving. I don't want to sound too good to be human but I reckon it could cost me a lot of sales.'

'Oh?'

He nodded. 'Look at it this way. If I'd let fly at that fellow I'd have started the habit for the day. By the time I get to my first call I'll probably have cursed ten drivers and I'll be in a pretty fair old state. Then perhaps my first housewife is difficult, and if she really gets on my wick then the next ten drivers are in for a heck of a time—and so on. By the end of the day I'm as cantankerous as a bitch with fleas and this is only Monday! By Wednesday I'm feeling mad at the world even before I get out of bed and by Friday I just can't live with myself. Now, you can imagine how I'm going to appear to the clients, can't you? I'd be lucky to do five machines a week.'

I nodded and grinned sheepishly at him. 'Point taken, mate.'

'It's worth remembering,' he said.

We got out of town and into a suburb called Wavertree. Eventually we found the road for the first call. It was a quiet, narrow one full of small, neat terraced houses.

'Number eighteen, isn't it?' said Jim.

I checked the lead slip. 'Yes.'

He pulled up outside number eight.

'No, eighteen, Jim,' I said.

He nodded. 'Just a fad of mine. I like to park a bit away from the house and have a look at the neighbourhood first—you know, just to get in the right frame of mind for selling.'

I was beginning to see why he was top salesman most weeks.

'What sort of person d'you think lives in this street?' he said.

I looked at the houses. They were tiny three-bedroom jobs with no frontage at all and probably an outside loo in the backyard.

'Certainly working class,' I said.

He nodded. 'Rent—thirty bob a week. No garages, no cars in the street. Not one of them too well off so the women will do a lot of sewing, patching—you know, making do. Mrs Kennedy will probably have an old machine to trade in.'

He saw my question coming and beat me to it.

'Oh, I know, we ask about that inside, but it makes a bit of difference if you're prepared for the answer. It gives you that little bit more confidence that comes across to the customer.'

I shook my head in admiration. 'You really work at it, Jim, don't you?'

He looked a little surprised. 'Of course—it's my living. Come on, let's go and chat Mrs Kennedy.'

She was a jolly little body, wrinkled before her time by the slog of domestic drudgery and the constant manipulation of housekeeping to make ends meet; but it hadn't got her down. Her figure had gone for a loop but her spirit was very much intact.

She bustled around, settling us comfortably in her tiny rear room and insisting on putting the kettle on before she would listen to a word. And while she was in the kitchen Jim chatted long-distance to her and found out that she had three children and an old Singer treadle.

While the kettle boiled, Jim whistled through the dem on the Minor and sold it like a shot. Then she took down the tea caddy from the high mantelpiece and gave him five one pound notes as easy as that.

As she jumped up to make the tea, Jim asked her if she'd heard our special offer on commercial radio and when she said no, I darted out to his car and brought in the Major. You should have seen her face when he took the cover off. She was like a hungry orphan in a pie shop.

Well, I won't clatter on about what followed because, believe me, it went almost word for word as it had done in the mock dem between Jim and O'Neill in the shop. It was uncanny. She threw in exactly the same objections as O'Neill had done about the price and having to speak to her husband and so on, but Jim just ploughed on in a nice quiet, polite way, and, hey presto, before you could say anti-disestablishmentarianism she'd bought it.

It was the trade-in offer that clinched it, because only a few days before a rag-and-bone man had offered her ten bob top wack for her old treadle and the five pounds that Jim offered was just too good to miss.

We had a lovely cup of tea afterwards and she couldn't wait to close the front door and get back to her new toy.

Back in the car I was really chuffed about the sale but Jim was very calm about it all.

'But it worked, Jim ... !' I said, '... just like the dem with O'Neill.'

'Naturally,' he drawled, with an extra helping of nonchalance, just for a joke. 'Did you ever doubt it?' Then he laughed. 'No, seriously, Russ, that was a gift. They come an awful lot tougher than that—otherwise we'd all be doing fifty machines a week, wouldn't we?' He put the car into gear and drove back to the main road. 'In a way,' he said, 'although it would've cut my throat—I wish that'd been a tougher one, just to start you off.' He turned his head and grinned at me. 'Never mind, we'll get a right bitch before the week's out, I promise you.'

Well, we had to wait until Thursday for his bitch, but when she did finally come along she was a beaut.

It was our last call on Thursday afternoon and it took us right back to the Scotland Road slums, which fact delighted me not at all. This time, though, it wasn't to a tenement but to a house, a sad, dirty-faced little effort in a bleak, cobbled street of endless terraced similars. As we turned into the street I shivered and pulled my overcoat closer to me. Gaslight glistened on the pavement, wet from the afternoon rain, and a stiff icy breeze rippled the shallow puddles trapped between the stone sets in the road.

Jim seemed quite undeterred.

We pulled to the curb and as he cut the engine the children arrived from nowhere. Twenty of them surrounded the car as menacingly as head-hunters; tots stared wide-eyed and wiped leaking noses on woolly sleeves and the older ones glowered covetously at the hub-caps, the wing mirrors and the wipers.

I expected Jim to clear them off or at least warn them as Vince had done but instead he smiled at them and crouched down in front of one tot in an appalling floral dress and offered his hand.

'Hello, what's your name?' he said with a big smile.

The child pouted and fidgetted and for a moment I thought she was going to run away but then, slowly, Jim's smile won her over and she began to smile back at him shyly.

The others were crowding round in a tight circle, craning their necks to see what was happening.

'Come on, what's your name?' Jim said again.

The child didn't answer but a dozen voices shouted, 'Janie . . . 'er name's Janie, mister.'

Jim stood up and looked at the kids. At the back of the pack was a scowling, eight-year-old heavyweight who was eyeing the car as though he was plotting to vivisect it as soon as we disappeared. His eyes shifted to Jim and belligerently held the stare in spite of Jim's smile.

'Hi!' said Jim. 'What's your name?'

The boy dropped his eyes and said, 'Jack,' scraping the word gutterally from the back of his throat.

'Come here, Jack . . . please.'

The kid pushed through the group reluctantly and looked up at Jim with suspicion. Jim put his hand lightly on the boy's shoulder and pulled him a bit nearer.

'You must be the leader, Jack, is that right?'

Jack swelled visibly with authority. 'Yes,' he said gruffly.

'Well, now, how would you like to do a job for me?'

Suspicion narrowed the little fellow's eyes and for a moment he looked as shrewd and experienced as a grown man.

'Warrisit?' he said.

Jim turned round and patted his car. 'While I'm in the house talking to Mrs Onslow I want you and your gang to keep an eye on my car and make sure no kids from the other streets do any damage to it.' He looked around at the children who were all gazing up at him and trying to work out what fiddle he was on.

'I know you wouldn't do it any harm,' he went on, 'because this is your street and you know Mrs Onslow, but some other kids might come along and write on it or scratch it and I want you all to stand guard on it. Will you do that for me?'

' 'Ow much?' said Jack.

He'd go far, this child.

'Two bob,' said Jim, '—for sweets for all the kids.'

' 'Alf a dollar,' insisted Jack.

Jim held out his hand and shook Jack's grubby paw.

'It's a deal,' he laughed.

We got the Minor out of the boot and knocked on the door. Mrs Onslow was a nervous, sad-eyed creature, skinny as a hairpin and really bashed about by life—and not only by life, it seemed; under her right eye was a bright purple mouse that had been the terminus for a good solid bunch of knuckles. I felt my stomach turn over.

As we went into the dark hallway I could hear young Jack flinging orders to the kids, posting them around the car with warnings of instant massacration if they failed to protect it. Jim turned and grinned at me but I wasn't in a grinning mood. I was beginning to feel nervous. There was something about the house and about Mrs Onslow that was giving me a strengthy premonition of danger and disaster.

Mrs Onslow shut out the sounds of the street and then the smell hit me again. It wasn't as strong as the tenement pong but it was unmistakably the same—the odour of ancient poverty. I wanted to go home right then and have a bath.

She squeezed past us and led us into the depressing back room. Automatically her sense of hospitality took her to the big iron kettle which had been removed from the open grate and put on one side.

'Cuppa tea?' she said, but in a lifeless, preoccupied sort of way.

'Er ... that's very kind of you, Mrs Onslow...' said Jim, grimacing at me, '... but we've just finished one. Thanks all the same. Now...'

He looked at the dining table and winced. It was crammed full of all sorts of junk from breakfast dishes to a pair of men's pyjamas which she'd obviously been mending when we knocked on the door.

'I wonder if we could...' said Jim.

79

'Oh, yes . . . I'm sorry . . .'

She bundled the lot off into the back kitchen and made a big effort to sponge the table down but most of the stains just had a quiet giggle and stayed put. Well, eventually Jim got under way with the dem but I could tell his heart wasn't in it somehow. Perhaps he realized that she wouldn't be able to afford the Major in a month of August Bank Holidays and that the whole thing was a great waste of time; or perhaps he just wanted to get out of the smelly hole as much as I did. Well, he was trundling along half-heartedly with the dem when suddenly we began to hear the commotion out in the street. It was nothing specific at first, just a lot of shouting and a man's deep voice booming out as if he was chasing our kids away, but Mrs Onslow knew what it was all about all right. The poor soul froze and all the colour drained out of her face and then she started shaking.

'Oh, dear . . .' she said, wringing her hands together and looking around the room as if she was trying to find somewhere to hide.

'What's the matter?' asked Jim, and I could tell from his voice that he'd picked up the danger signals just as I had when I first came into the place. I knew what Mrs Onslow was going to say before she said it.

'It's . . . my husband . . .' she said weakly. 'I was hoping you were going to call earlier . . . before he . . .'

We heard the key grating in the front door and then it opened and we could hear the kids shouting and jeering out in the street.

'Garn, bugger off, you kids or I'll lay the belt on yer,' shouted the man and the house seemed to shake with the power of his voice. Then it really did shake as the door slammed shut and his footsteps thundered down the hallway.

The door burst open and the gigantic Irish navvy stood there filling the frame while he got his eyes in focus and started sorting us all out. He was built like a side of beef and was skinned to his eyeballs in Guinness. First he caught sight of me and he began looking at me just as Gladys, the alsatian, had done—wondering which of my limbs to rip off and devour first; then he let his bloody, piggy eyes sidle over to Jim, then to the machine and then, finally, to his wife. God, how he looked at her!

Slowly a wicked, vicious smile slipped into his face and he took a step into the room.

'Well now, isn't this cosy,' he said, his soft, deep, rumbling voice making the cups rattle in their saucers. 'What's it all about, Nellie?'

'Joe ... I ... I ...'

'Spit it out, chuck,' he said, his voice getting less easy.

I just sat there paralysed, wishing to God that Jim and I were just driving over the border into Scotland.

'Mr Onslow, perhaps I can ...' said Jim.

'Shut up, you!' roared Onslow and thrust his prestressed concrete fist at Jim's hooter.

'Joe!' yelled the brave little woman. 'Leave these two alone! I asked them to come round ...'

Onslow let his glare slide slowly off Jim and on to his wife. 'Oh,' he said, quiet again now. 'You asked them to come round ...'

There was a long, deep silence in the little room that was as pregnant with disaster as the moment before a ten-day naval barrage. Onslow flicked his eyes between Jim and me several times more and I swore to Heaven that if ever I got out of that house alive I would take up Karate and Judo and Akaido and Yawara and Ate-waza and Savate and always, always carry on my person a sten-gun and a revolver and a hand-grenade and an assortment of knives, clubs, blackjacks and knuckledusters together with aerosol cans of tear-gas and instant anaesthetic and ...

'Get out!' Onslow said quietly.

We got.

'So you see,' said Jim, swallowing his second Scotch in one gulp, 'selling isn't all a bed of Dunlopillo.'

I lifted my glass, trying to make light of the twitching and trembling that was still going on all over my body.

'Point taken,' I said. 'Have another.'

We had several and by Friday morning I was beginning to feel a bit better.

NINE

'There she is, Jim,' said Bob Butler. 'And she's not bad ... not bad at all.'

The three of us walked into the workshop where a young lad in overalls was giving the Hillman a final wipe down and I felt the excitement jump inside me as I clapped eyes on it for the first time.

'We've put in a new cylinder-head gasket and one new tyre,' said Butler. 'The rest seems very good.' He grinned at me. 'Not exactly a D.B.5, Russ, but it'll do you until you can afford to graduate.'

I walked around the little beauty and ran my fingers gently over its smart-looking gun-metal blue paintwork and shining chrome.

'It looks terrific,' I said.

Butler nodded like the expert he was. 'Yes, she's been looked after. It belonged to a woman and they do tend to take care of things better than we do, don't they?'

I opened the door and sat in the driver's seat and tested the pedals and the steering wheel. The interior looked and smelled clean, with the faintest trace of the woman's perfume still lingering in the upholstery as though it was reluctant to leave. Well, with a bit of luck, I reflected lecherously, it'd have a bit of company before too long.

As a projection of this line of thought I swivelled round and had a gander at the back seat. Well, not too spacious, but with a little co-operation, a little bit of give and take ...

'Like a spin?' said Butler.

He opened the door and I moved over to the passenger seat and Jim Stanford got in the back. I thought it was ruddy nice of Jim to give me his time like this. I told him he'd done enough for me already but he insisted on coming along and seeing the thing through.

We didn't drive far, just through town and back again but Butler gave her the gun whenever he could to show me what the engine was like, and I thought it was pretty fair.

'Bit of tappet noise,' Butler said honestly, 'but that's to be expected.'

We got back to the garage and Butler slid away diplomatically while Jim and I compared notes.

'I think you've got yourself a car, Russ,' he said. 'I don't think you'll better that for a hundred and fifty.'

So we clinched the deal. Jim left us to load his car up with machines and Butler got down to filling in the H.P. forms and arranging a cover note for the insurance. It was all done in half an hour.

'You'll pick it up tonight, Russ?' he said. 'We're open till eight on Fridays so she'll be here waiting for you when you knock off.'

Well, I think you know just how Friday dragged along for me. Even the fact of Jim selling three machines couldn't budge my mind from that Hillman just sitting there waiting for me.

I thought I was hiding it pretty well until Jim said, 'I know just how you feel, Russ. I was exactly the same with my first car but I had to wait a week to collect mine. Drove me nuts.'

He looked at me sideways and grinned. 'Where to tonight? A little maiden spin up to Edinburgh?'

I laughed. 'A "maiden" spin, yeh, but not to Edinburgh. I think I'll let it show itself off to a lady mate of mine.'

'That's the idea, boy—don't let it stand idle at the kerb. You make it earn its keep.'

At lunchtime I phoned Gloria and just caught her before she left the office. She gave a little yelp of delight when I told her about the car.

'Oh, Russ,' she said, 'I'm so glad for you. When am I going to see it?'

'Well, I thought maybe tonight if . . .'

'Oh, yes! Come round and have dinner.'

'Mm?'

'Come round early and I'll cook you something . . .' she laughed, '. . . beans or something. I'm gorgeous at beans.'

My cup was running over all over the place, I can tell you. What more could a man want? An interesting job that paid real money, a car to call his own, and a sweet, sexy pet like Gloria. I felt like jumping over the P. & O. building.

The afternoon passed in a series of resplendent daydreams, each one more lavish, more pulchritudinous than the last. I'd done so many outrageous things by five o'clock that I felt quite exhausted—but not for long. As I stepped out of Jim's car at Butler's garage I felt like a stud bull with two whatsits. I said goodnight to Jim who gave me a big wink and drove off laughing and I went into the garage.

'There she is, Russ,' said Butler. 'She's all yours and the best of luck with the machines. And don't forget, if you have any trouble just bring it in and we'll see you're all right.'

He handed me the papers and opened the door ceremoniously for me.

'Starter, lights, windshield wipers, choke . . .' he said, pointing at the things. 'You know the gears?'

I turned the key, pressed the starter and the mighty engine roared out its indescribable power—well, that's what it seemed like to me—and I was away!—straight into the five o'clock traffic jam.

She handled like a dream. I was Jim Clark all the way up Brownlow Hill, Stirling Moss along Wavertree Road and by the time I reached Childwall I was eighty-five laps ahead of the field with an average speed of a hundred and forty-seven miles an hour. Actually, the five-mile journey took nearly half an hour.

I leapt out of the car and pressed Gloria's door bell with a flourish, intending to sweep her away for a quick flip before tea. There was no answer. Of course, fool, she didn't get home till six.

I sat in the car feeling damned superior and really believing that all the girls who walked past were just dying to leap in beside me; and then, would you believe it, a bloke parked in front of me in a bright red Jaguar. So I backed down the street a bit.

I saw Gloria get off the bus and I gave her a toot. She looked around with a very frozen bit of brush-off and, stap me, I had to wind down the window and give her a call. She spun round, gaped, and then came running over.

'Oh, Russ,' she laughed as she jumped in, showing me all sorts of thigh that started me off quicker than Piggott in the Derby, 'I thought it was someone being fresh.'

'It was,' I said, giving her a little kiss.

'You're not fresh, lover,' she cooed. 'You're welcome.' She gave me not such a little kiss back and then looked around the car.

'Russ, it's gorgeous, it really is!'

'Like it?' I said nonchalantly.

'Love it! Love the colour, love the design, love the driver!'

'Shucks,' I said.

She snuggled up, all excited. 'Where shall we go?'

I pretended to think. 'Well now, how about Nice, Madrid, Lisbon and Rome and then somewhere else after dinner?'

She dug me in the ribs and then her hand fell dangerously near Prince Richard without actually touching him.

'I've missed you in the office,' she said seriously. 'The old dump just hasn't been the same.'

I smiled at her because I knew she meant it and kissed her on the forehead.

'What's my replacement like?'

She shrugged and pulled a face. 'Not much. Young, handsome, rich. We neck during the lunch hour but it's not the same.'

I laughed out loud and gave her a tickle.

'Come on,' I said, 'let's just cruise around a bit and feel opulent.'

It was getting dark by then as it does in March so I flicked on the lights and we cruised down Childwall Valley and did a long circuit for about half an hour. Oh, it was nice. This was really living. To be leaping along with the cold wind shut out and Gloria all warm and cuddly tucked into my left side.

I told her all about the two weeks at Ritebuy and about Vince and Charlie and the lads and randy old Draper and the smells and Joe Onslow (she blinkin'-well giggled about that!) and about how good Jim Stanford had been and about Mrs Henderson's wild birthday party. She gave my arm a squeeze and said, 'Oh, I'm so glad you like it, Russ. You sound different, you know. I can tell you're happy there. I think you'll sell thousands.'

'Thanks, honey. Well, starting Monday, I'm going to give it a darn good try.'

We got back to her place and of course we didn't have beans for dinner. She cooked me a marvellous mixed grill and we had a drop of six and ninepenny Yugoslav Riesling with it and it was all delicious.

Afterwards I gave her a hand with the washing up and broke a plate so she ordered me to sit down and then she came in all prettied up and sat on my knee. But not for long. In front of her fireplace, which had a nice rosy-glowing fire in it, was a white sheepskin rug . . .

Until then I'd never made love on a sheepskin rug in front of a nice rosy-glowing fire on a cold night in March. And to all those who also have not but who are in a position to try it—do yourselves a favour.

Saturday morning—my last day as a trainee.

I drove down to Ritebuy like the Duke of Fazakerly and swept into the yard. All the lads made complimentary noises about the Hillman and even Draper and Sands came out to have a gander at the finest car in the north of England.

'That'll do fine,' said Sands. 'Just fine, Russ. Oh, pop in and see me when you've finished with Jim, will you. We'll have a chat about next week.'

Reluctantly I left the old girl in the yard while I did the morning with Jim. Once on the road he gave me a sneaky grin and said, 'Well?'

I gave him a very self-satisfied look and said, 'Very' and he burst out laughing.

'You christened it?'

'Oh, no,' I said disdainfully. 'I mean, the back seat's strictly the last resort, isn't it? Comfort's my middle name.'

Jim took up the joke and nodded seriously. 'You're right, mate. This "one leg in the steering wheel and the other in the boot" business is for kids. We men of the world, we ... er ... how old are you?'

'Twenty-two.'

'. . . we men of the world, we artists, if you like, we need space to create, room to expose ourselves, our subtleties, and you can't do those things with your bum in the ashtray, can you?'

I agreed.

'. . . and, besides, it can be dangerous. I had a mate who had to pull out quick one night and goosed himself severely on the window winder.'

It wasn't true, of course, but we had a good laugh.

We finished the morning and back at the yard I thanked Jim for all his help and promised him a quadruple Scotch up at the cricket club the next time up there. Then he drove home and I went in to see Jimmy Sands.

'Well, Russ,' he said, 'how d'you think you'll make out?'

I told him I thought I'd be all right.

'Splendid. Well, we'll start you off on Monday and you have our blessings. If you do as well at selling as you did with Charlie you'll make a fortune. Have a good week-end.'

I thanked him and walked back across the yard just as the last of the salesmen were leaving. I waved cheerio to them, unlocked the Hillman, and just sat there for a few minutes, thinking about Monday and about Gloria and a few odd bits and pieces. And then, there was Jimmy Sands tearing across the yard as though his Y-fronts were on fire, waving a piece of paper in the air as he came.

'Russ!' he gasped, 'thank Heaven you haven't gone. Here ... how ... would you like to make your first sale?'

I just stared at him.

'... just had a telephone call ... chap saw our ad in this morning's paper ... his daughter's getting married this afternoon ... wants a sewing machine for her ... sounds a bit of a foreigner ... wants a dem at four o'clock ... should be a cert!'

He thrust the paper into my hand.

'There's the address. Think you can do it, boy? Come on into the stockroom.'

'Er ...'

'Good boy! Do you the world of good! Come and get the machines.'

He shot back across the yard and I followed, my heart thumping like a fire pump. This was too soon! I wasn't prepared. I was going to start on Monday!

When I got to the stockroom Sands was closing the catches on a Minor.

'That one's O.K.,' he said and reached for a Major.

He inspected it and O.K.'d that and thrust it at me.

'Right, put those in your car and come back for the papers and things.'

I trundled off to the Hillman and stowed the machines away and then went back. He was holding a battered leather briefcase in one hand and shoving H.P. papers and dem cloths and things into it with the other.

'There you are ... receipt book, H.P. papers, cloths ... all there. Got a pen? Good boy. Got the address? Splendid. Right, go to it, Russ, and see if you can't sell your first machine. Good luck, I'll see you on Monday.'

I was in a right stew, I can tell you. I don't think a trapeze artist with a bee in his ear could've been more nervous. I drove out of the yard feeling all cold and shivery like I do in the dentist's waiting room and for about ten minutes I hadn't a clue where I was driving. I just drove automatically while awful pictures of failure raced through my head—pictures of Joe Onslow and pictures of being thrown downstairs and pictures of me seizing up altogether and forgetting the dem.

And then I found myself down by the river at the Pier Head.

I parked the car and stepped out into the cold wind that was blowing up from New Brighton and I started walking.

I must have wandered around for ten minutes before some common sense started penetrating my noodle. What the heck was I worried about? I knew the machines and I knew the dem, didn't I? Damn it, I'd just spent a whole week with Ritebuy's best salesman so I should know what to do by now. In any case, even Jim Stanford didn't sell all his leads; even he had his failures. IF I met up with a Joe Onslow—which was highly unlikely at a wedding, for Pete's sake—then I'd just have to do what Jim Stanford did—retire gracefully. And IF I didn't make a sale, well, who was going to ball me out? What could they do? Peg me out on Seacombe sand and leave me to the crabs?

I gave myself a right dressing down and no messing. I felt ashamed of myself. By Heaven, come Monday—which was only two days away—I was going to start doing this for a living and then I couldn't afford to behave like a virgin about to break her duck.

I went back to the car and looked up the address in my street map. There, you see, you great twoddle, it was a nice area for a start—so no Joe Onslow to worry about. I was beginning to feel much better.

I started the car and began driving towards the house—which was in a place called Aigburth—going over the dem in my mind. On the way I found a little cafe and I sat in the corner and had a good talk to myself over eggs and chips and three cups of tea.

Half past three. I paid the waitress and went back to the car. I thought I'd arrive early, make sure of finding the house so I couldn't be late.

I found it all right. Oh, it was a nice house, nothing wrong with it at all, but it wasn't what it was but where it was that turned my stomach over. It was on the top of a hill! You know the kind of thing—fifty steps up from the pavement and as sheer as the north face of the Eiger. There was a driveway leading up to the garage, but this was jam-packed with wedding cars and there were so many of them that about ten were parked in the street in front of the house, so I couldn't even get near the front gate! Now, you see, this is the sort of thing that would never happen in a million years if I'd been with Jim Stanford or Tom O'Neill and here it was happening on my very first solo dem. How in blazes was I going to 'nip' out and get the Major once I'd sold the Minor? You just can't 'nip' down fifty steps, walk a quarter of a mile to your car and then 'nip' up them again lugging forty pounds three ounces of sewing machine under your arm. It'd take you a day to get your breath back.

Disaster was imminent, I could taste it. I felt sick. That was it—I'd go sick! Sands would be disappointed on Monday but he'd understand. A bad chip in the cafe! Food poisoning. A brave attempt to climb the fifty steps but complete blackout on the forty-third.

The disgusted ghosts of Jim Stanford and Gloria stirred in the back seat. Chicken-hearted twit, they whispered. Cowardy, cowardy custard! I felt ashamed. Go to it, boy! Get up them stairs and sell!

I took a deep breath and leapt from the car. With my Minor in one hand and my briefcase in the other I ran up the first twenty steps, walked up the next twenty and staggered up the final ten. By the time I got to the top I was finished—and the Minor weighs less than half the Major!

I put the Minor down and sat on it for half a minute, listening to the blood rushing along my arteries like a tidal wave in a sewer pipe. But half a minute wasn't long enough. The front door opened suddenly and a nice little thing in blue satin and a funny little hat nearly walked into my face.

'Hello!' she said, her eyes popping.

I shot up.

'Sorry,' I gasped. 'It's the ... the steps ...'

She grinned demurely. 'Yes, they are a bit of a bastard, aren't they?'

She was gorgeous. Long blonde hair sweeping over her right eye and a pair of full, very edible lips smiling away over perfect teeth, moist, warm and welcoming. And the figure! Two lush, satin-skinned grapefruits fighting their way out of the dress that was cut so low you could almost see the pips. And did she smell good! All fresh and clean and perfumed as though she'd just that minute stepped out of a shower. Now there was a thought to swill around and swallow.

'What can I do for you?' she said, looking me up and down.

'Er ... er ...' What in blazes were the words? 'Er ... my name is Russ Tobin ...'

'Nice,' she said.

'I'm from ... er ... Ritebuy Sewing Machines ...'

89

'Lucky old Ritebuy,' she said, laughing at me. 'Come in, Russ Tobin.'

I squeezed past her because she made me do it and stepped into bedlam. You should have seen it. There must have been fifty thousand people in the hall alone and another million on the stairs. Nobody took a blind bit of notice of me because they were all talking eighty-four to the dozen and drinking champagne and generally having an hilarious time. Blondie came up behind me and took my arm like we were engaged or something and gave it a squeeze.

'My name's Samantha,' she said. 'Come into the kitchen.'

We pushed our way through the party dresses and the lounge suits and by the time we got to the kitchen only two glasses of bubbly had been spilled down my mac, which was pretty good going, believe me. But if I'd expected the kitchen to be any sort of refuge from the turmoil, I was mistaken. It was large and beautifully fitted out and was accommodating about ten more people than there were in the hall. There was a big table in the centre groaning with eating-and-drinking-type goodies—jellies, blancmanges, sandwiches, tit-bits and fancies, and every conceivable type of booze.

'Have a drink,' shouted Samantha.

Well, she had to shout because besides all the chat that was going on there was an extension speaker on the wall that was doing its level best to shatter everybody's ear drums with Stan Kenton's 'Peanut Vendor' or the '1812 Overture' or something.

'Er ...'

'Good,' she yelled and poured me a tumbler of bubbly. 'Who did you want to see?' she shouted.

'Pardon?'

'Oh ...' She frowned at the loudspeaker and beckoned my ear towards those incredible lips. I bent down and got her warm, sweet breath in my ear and found myself staring straight down her voluptuous cleavage. She knew it too and didn't mind a bit.

'Wwhhoo ...' she went, blowing right into my earhole, '... wwhhoo did you want to see?'

I felt big goose-bumps break out all over my body like my skin was falling off and I shivered. Samantha laughed.

'Pardon?' I said.

This time she killed herself laughing and when she tried to repeat the 'wwhhoo' she couldn't for laughing. Instead she slipped her hand under my arm and gave it a squeeze.

'Oh, I like you, Russ Tobin,' she shouted. 'Now, seriously, who did you come to see?'

'Mr ... er ...' I'd forgotten the name so I had to get the piece of paper out of my pocket. 'Mr Renowski.'

'He's my uncle,' she said. 'Mary's my cousin—it's her wedding.'

'Where is he?' I asked.

Oh, those eyes. They never stopped teasing and promising for a minute.

She shrugged. 'Let's go and find him. Are you going to sell him this?' She nodded at the Minor on the floor.

'I hope so.'

'So—let's go and find him.'

I watched her wiggle away in front of me with the satin dress doing the samba across her beautiful bottom and I followed it.

We found Uncle Renowski surrounded by six obvious relatives all talking to him at once. The poor little fellow looked demented. Samantha fought her way through and whispered in his ear and without so much as a shiver he looked up and nodded at me and started to excuse himself through the crowd.

'Ah, Mr ... er ...'

'Tobin.'

'Mr Tobin ... good of you to come. I'm sorry about the ...' he flapped his podgy hand at the furore, '... but Hungarian weddings are like this, you know.'

'So are English ones,' I said.

'Good,' he said, not really knowing what he was saying. 'Now ... if you have the machine? I'm not at all sure, mind you, that this is the right one for Mary but it's cheap enough and it might do her for a while. Where is it?'

'It's in the kitchen,' I said, getting all panicky now. 'Er ... do you have a fairly large table, Mr Renowski?'

He looked at me as though I'd asked him if he had a hernia. 'A large table? What for, young man?'

There you go, you see. Jim Stanford never had this trouble in the entire week I was with him. People always had a large table for Jim and always knew what he wanted it for.

'Well, to demonstrate the machine on,' I said.

'How big is it?' laughed Renowski. 'I don't want a combine harvester, you know—only a sewing machine.'

We were pushing our way through to the kitchen all this

91

time and talking to each other through people's ears.

'But I'm sure you'd like a bit of space to work...'

Well, that was bloody daft for a start! I couldn't exactly see Renowski sitting down in the middle of this lot and running up a few bits and pieces for Mary's bottom drawer. What was worse, I couldn't even see myself sitting down to dem the damned thing.

'I beg your pardon?' he said.

Fortunately we got separated at this point by a tray of champagne coming out of the kitchen and I didn't bother to resume the line of conversation afterwards.

'Here it is,' I said, picking up the Minor and looking around for somewhere to put it.

'Here—on the draining board,' said Renowski.

On the drain board!

'Er ... is there a plug,' I said, feeling quite faint.

'Yes,' said Renowski, really baffled now. He picked up the plug out of the sink and waved it around on the chain. 'You want some water, maybe?'

I laughed. 'No, I meant an electric plug—for the machine.'

'Oh,' he said, looking round the kitchen.

There was a cluster of three outlets over some low cupboards but the working surface was crammed with jellies and glasses and it was all too impossible for words.

Renowski shrugged and smiled apologetically. 'Why for do you want a plug, anyhow?'

'Well ... to ... demonstrate the machine,' I said patiently.

Renowski smiled and shook his head. 'Oh, no, not to bother yourself. I'm sure it will work beautifully, otherwise you would not be here selling it, would you? No, just let me see it, if you please.'

'Yes ... certainly,' I said weakly, knowing now that I'd been dead right about that feeling of pending disaster. You see, Jim ... Gloria, I wasn't just being chicken. I just knew this was going to happen. Now all I could do was hope he'd take one look at it, let out a yowl of disgust and kick me and the Minor down the steps.

I smelled Samantha at my elbow and looked round into her twinkling eyes. She gave me a wink that sent a tingle all the way down to my Italian casuals and then she looked expectantly at the Minor.

I whipped the lid off and waited for the outburst.

'Ha, a lovely little fellow,' beamed Renowski. 'So compact

'... so light ... and so cheap!'

Hey, those are my lines, Renowski.

'A bit small, isn't it?' murmured the delightful Samantha.

Go on, Sam, smash it to bits ... kill the sale ... let me go home.

'... it's what they call a three-quarter head, sir,' I found myself saying. 'Yes, it is, as you say, compact, light and very inexpensive ...'

'I like it, young man. We'll have it.'

Oh, my sainted aunt.

'Thank you very much, sir. Oh, by the way, did you happen to hear our special offer on commercial radio this morning?'

Renowski looked at me as though I'd just shouted 'knickers' at the top of my voice.

'You must be joking, young man,' he said. 'This place has been a lunatic asylum since five o'clock this morning. I can't imagine anything less likely than I should be listening to special offers on commercial radio.'

'No, of course not,' I laughed, feeling a right berk. 'Well, would you excuse me for a moment, sir ...'

'Yes, certainly. Er ... Samantha, show Mr Trowbridge where it is, will you, darling ...'

Samantha grinned at me and took my arm. 'Top of the stairs, first on the left ...'

'Oh, no ...' I protested. 'I didn't ... I mean I wasn't going to the toilet. I was going out to my car.'

Renowski frowned. 'What for?'

'Well, to show you our special offer ...'

'What is it?'

'It's a sewing machine ... a big one ... it's incredible value, really ...'

Renowski now thought I'd really lost my slates and I can't say I blame him.

'But I've just bought a machine,' he laughed. 'What would I want with two?'

'Yes, precisely ...' I said. 'That's just it, you see. I can't sell it to you, can I, because you've just bought one. But we get paid a commission to demonstrate it so that you can tell your friends and ...'

Renowski was looking around him nervously and I think it was for a strait-jacket.

'Excuse me, Mr Rolands, but I must see to my guests. Samantha, get Mr Rolands a drink, darling, and also the

93

receipt for the five pounds, there's a good girl. Very nice to have met you, Mr Rolands, and thank you very much for coming round.' He was heading away towards the lounge. 'Make yourself at home,' he shouted over his shoulder.

Samantha collapsed. 'You should see your face!' she laughed. 'I've never seen anything so miserable...'

And I was feeling miserable, I can tell you. I'm willing to bet a year's commission (which, come to think of it, will be sweet F.A. at this rate) that this situation has never happened to any one of the lads at Ritebuy since the firm was founded. Everything, every single thing I'd learned over the past fortnight, absolutely useless! Not one argument had applied, not one principle had pertained. Not even a chance to kill the rotten sale! Well, Sands and Draper and O'Neill and Ritebuy and the whole bunch of them could spifflicate themselves if I got one word of criticism about this little lot. I felt like getting drunk.

Samantha must have read the intent in my miserable face.

'Here, here's your champagne,' she said. 'Though I don't know what you're so miserable about—you sold it, didn't you?'

I swallowed half the tumbler and felt the bubbly gurgling down into my tum.

'You don't understand...' I began saying and then decided I'd better shut up.

'Oh, yes I do,' she said knowingly. 'You were trying to pull a switch.'

I gaped at her.

'A what?'

'Oh, come off it, Russ darling. I know all about it. My brother does it.'

'Does what?'

She sighed. 'Sells on the "switch"—but he does it with cars. He advertises a good bargain and when you get there to buy it it's just been snapped up. But, by pure chance, he just happens to have a slightly more expensive one...'

I looked into her teasing eyes and I started to laugh. And then we were both killing ourselves and all the tension and worry was running out of me and from that moment we started having a marvellous time.

At about half past five we were sitting on the stairs and I was getting as tiddly as a wink and yacking to everybody in sight but really I was watching Samantha. I really fancied this one and she knew it and was giving me a real subtle going over—touching me, smiling at me, showing me bits of her gorgeous body, flirting outrageously.

She brought her mouth down to my ear and whispered, 'Wwhhhere do you live, Russ?'

There, she was doing it again—blowing her h's into my ear and playing havoc with my composure.

'Anfield,' I said.

'Alone?'

And I thought it was always the lads who asked these questions.

I shook my head. 'No, I've got a room in a boarding house.'

She pouted and made me feel a right twit for not having a sumptuous flat and a wall-to-wall mattress.

'You've got a car though, haven't you?' she said.

Ah, now this was better.

'Oh, yes,' I said casually.

She slipped her hand under my arm and came in even closer. 'Take me for a ride,' she whispered.

'Now?'

'Why not?'

'Well, what about . . .' I waved at the people.

'Oh, this'll go on for hours. Mary's upstairs having a bit of a lie down. She won't be down for an hour yet.'

'Well, sure,' I said. 'I'd love to.'

'I'll get my coat,' she whispered. 'You slip out now and wait for me at the bottom of the steps.'

My heart was thumping like the clappers. I squeezed through to the front door and went down the steps. On the pavement I did a lot of deep breathing to get rid of some of the champagne but it seemed to make it worse. After a couple of minutes Samantha came tripping down from the heights like a prima ballerina and flung her arm into mine.

'Let's get away from the crowd for a bit,' she said. 'It's like Butlins in there. Where's your car?'

I did the gentlemanly thing and opened the door for her and she rewarded me with an eyeful of stocking-tops.

'Where to?' I said, getting in.

She smiled mysteriously and said, 'Sefton Park Gate.'

'Where's that?'

'Drive on—I'll show you. Turn right at the end of the road.'

Well now, I'll tell you where Sefton Park Gate was—or

rather what it was. It was her house! Momma had brought Sonny Jim home.

It was a nice place, too. Fairly big and modern with enough garden to have several games of croquet going at the same time without hitting someone else's ball.

'Er . . . I'd just park down the road a bit,' she said and the alarums and excursions started jangling along the corridors of my tum.

We dumped the car and walked up the gravel path and she had the door open in a trice.

'Come in,' she said, so I did.

We went through to the lounge which was a lovely big room and very nicely done out. There was a white Indian carpet on the floor and a big comfy sofa with thick, squashy cushions on it. Samantha's mum and dad were not what you might call stuck for a bob exactly. Which thought brought to mind a question of some import.

'Where's your mother and father,' I asked casually.

She did a funny sort of smile and stretched her arms out wide and wrapped them right around her.

'We just left them—they were at the reception. They won't miss me, I promise, and they won't be home for hours.'

I felt my whole body kick over and start trembling like a jet-engine on a VC10 and my throat got all choked up. She was just begging to be kissed, so I kissed her. No, that's not exactly true either. It was more like falling into a warm, moist mincing machine and being sucked inside out. Then she stopped abruptly and whistled away across the room to draw the curtains. Then she was back at it again.

After a while she stopped again and danced over to the door.

'Make yourself comfortable, I'll be back,' she laughed, over her shoulder.

I dropped into the deep, squashy cushions and tried to stop my legs trembling. Then, after a few minutes when things were just beginning to get better, I heard her calling me. I went out to the hallway and saw her at the top of the stairs. She was leaning over the banister and her long blonde hair was falling over her face.

'Come up,' she said, and her voice choked a bit.

When I got to the top landing she was moving towards the rear bedroom and in the doorway she stopped, turned and crooked her index finger at me and the trembling started worse than ever.

The bedroom was all pink and feminine and smelled just like Samantha. I felt myself go dizzy with the soft perfume. By the bed was a tiny porcelain reading lamp which was throwing a nice quiet glow at the ceiling. I reckon that if Heaven looks like anything, it looks exactly like this room.

She had changed into a pink silk dressing gown and I could tell from the way her nips were standing out like acorns that she had nothing on underneath. She advanced on me slowly with a tigerish look in her eye and slipped her hands under my jacket. Then I fell into the mincer again and while all this was going on she was taking my clothes off.

The silk dressing gown slipped to the floor and we fell backwards on to the bed.

'I haven't . . . got anything,' I whispered.

She smiled a smile of complete self-assurance and took her mouth away just long enough to say, 'I was in the Guides, darling. I always come prepared.'

Then all hell broke loose.

It must have been the banging of the front door that woke us up. Samantha shot up in bed and I came round to an eyeful of those beautiful boobies.

'Samantha!' a man's voice called.

Then I shot up and I could see the panic in her eyes.

'My father!' she gasped.

'Samantha! Are you home, darling?'

'Oh, Christ,' I said.

Then, suddenly, she was in control of the situation. She put her finger to her lips and nipped out of bed, and believe me, even with all this panic going on I felt myself getting all worked up again at the sight of her. She was a naked knock-out.

She flung on the dressing gown and opened the door just a fraction.

'Hello, Daddy. Yes, I'm home.'

'Whasamarra, darlin'? We missed you at the party. Anything wrong?'

The old man sounded stoned.

She laughed. 'No, just a bit too much bubbly. I thought I'd come home and have a shower and then go back. I must have dropped off. What time is it?'

The old man seemed to be trying to find his watch.

'It's . . . it's . . . a quarter to eight, love.' I was thankful for that! I thought it was midnight.

'Where's Mother?' Samantha shouted down.

The old man cackled. 'She's lying down over there!' He went into pleats now. 'We were doing the Hokey Cokey and she fell asleep on one leg.'

I felt like laughing myself because I could feel the danger passing. Her father would never come into Samantha's room uninvited.

'I'm going to make a cup of tea, darlin',' he shouted. 'Would you like one? I'll bring one up, shall I?'

'Er . . . no thanks, Daddy. I'll be down soon.'

She closed the door and locked it and giggled at me.

'Lord, it must have been the champagne,' she laughed. 'We must have been asleep for an hour.'

She walked to the bed and flung herself across it and then rolled over on her back by my side. The dressing-gown cord parted with the movement and the gown opened wide—and I was off again.

In the heavenly calm that followed the shock wave she looked up at me all sleepy and satisfied and snuggled into my chest.

'You are beautiful at it,' she whispered. 'I've never been filled like that before.'

'Stop it,' I said, feeling very pleased with myself. 'You'll start me off again.'

'I believe I could, too,' she laughed, her fingers running up my thigh.

'You're damned right you could. I could do this for a week non-stop. It must be the champagne.'

She sighed and snuggled in again. 'Then we'll go away for a week sometime and take ten crates of champagne with us.'

'Wow!' I said, and took her hand away from where it didn't ought to have been just then.

'I must go,' I said reluctantly. 'How do I get out?'

She pouted and started playing games.

'I don't think I'm going to let you go. I think I'm going to keep you here for ever, locked in the wardrobe during the day and in here . . .' she took my hand and placed it on her tummy, '. . . all night. How would you like to be a kept man, Russ, baby?'

I gave her a kiss that told her exactly how the idea appealed to me and, so help me, she started coming to the boil again.

Well, it must have been after nine o'clock when her father

came trundling up the stairs and banged on her door.

'I'm off to bed, sweetie, or I'll never get up for church to-morrow. You all right?'

'Perfectly, Daddy,' she shouted and wrinkled her nose at me. 'Goodnight!'

'Goodnight, darlin'.'

It gives you a funny feeling, you know, lying in bed with a little pigeon when she's talking to her father through an eighth of an inch of wood. Sort of disrespectful or something.

'I'd better go,' I whispered and still she pouted but nodded her head at the same time.

'Yes, I suppose so, but ... oh ...' She wrapped herself round me and squeezed the air out of my chest. '... I don't want you to. I want you to sleep here all night.'

'There'll be other nights,' I said.

'There'd better be,' she threatened.

It still took me fifteen minutes to get my clothes on because after each garment we'd start necking again and at one point I had my shirt on and off again three times. Terrible, isn't it, how this love business gets you. And the effort you put into it! I reckon that enough energy is expended in love-making in any big city every night to run the power-stations for a month. I must work on that one. I might have discovered something quite revolutionary.

Anyway, I finally get my trousers zipped up—although that was touch and go for a while—and she eases the door open, and even from inside the room I could hear her father snoring his nose off along the landing, so I knew it was going to be easy. We slipped down the stairs and after about forty-two more goodnights by the front door I was actually outside. Samantha waved me off and closed the door and I was off down the driveway, breathing in the cold night air to dilute the sexy smog that was stuffing up my brain. And then, just as I was about to go out of the gate, a car drew up.

Would you believe it—two more seconds and I would've been outside and just another pedestrian. I looked around in the dark and spotted a clump of bushes just off the drive and I dived behind them feeling like Stan, Stan, the M.I.5 man.

The folks in the car were making a heck of a racket and it was apparent that Samantha's mum had arrived home. Three men got out of the car with her and held her up while they opened the gate and then they all linked arms and sang 'Show me the way to go home' in four different keys all the way to the front door.

Someone fumbled with a key and finally opened the door and Mrs Thingy shouted, 'Goodnight, Fred. Goodnight, Charlie. Goodnight, Alex. Goodnight . . .'

They got her in eventually and the three men came back down the drive laughing and coughing up nicotine and yacking about the wedding. And then, about three yards away, one said, 'Boy oh boy, do I need a slash. I'd better have one at Mag's before I drive home.'

He turned back towards the house but another fellow got hold of his sleeve and said, 'Nah, there's no need to bother them, Charlie. There's some bushes over there. Mag won't mind if we water her aspidistra.'

Now some of you might consider what followed to be humorous, but I think it goes without saying that I didn't. It was either put up or shut up for me and as I didn't fancy being dragged out by three half-cut blokes and ripped to shreds as a burglar I stuck it out. Believe me, that raincoat of mine has never been the same since. I had it dry-cleaned and re-texed six times, but I still didn't feel comfortable in it because I got the feeling that people were sort of sniffing at me and edging away when I was in a crowd and psychologically it was murdering my ego, so I ditched it. My dustman's wearing it now and good luck to him. Either his ego is more robust than mine or it's a simple case of ignorance being bliss. Anyway, it fits him so everybody's happy.

TEN

Came Monday—and what should have been an exciting, challenging day for me but which, of course, wasn't.

I got down to Ritebuy early, not only because of Jim Stanford's advice about getting loaded up first, but because I wanted to have a word with him about selling the Minor to Renowski. Jim was already in the yard when I drove up and I told him the whole story—well, nearly all of it!

He killed himself laughing, of course, especially about trying to dem on the draining board, and when he'd calmed down a bit he said, 'You poor old basket, fancy getting a dirty one like that for your first.'

We walked into the stockroom and started sorting out the machines.

'Ah, don't worry, Russ,' he said seriously. 'There's absolutely nothing anyone could've done in your place. I couldn't have done any better than you—short of slugging Renowski and making a run for it.'

'You really mean it, Jim?' I said, feeling a bit relieved.

'Well, hell yes,' he said. 'In the first place, you can't dem to a man, can you?—and certainly not to one half split on champagne when he's surrounded by eight thousand people at a wedding reception. Jimmy Sands should have known better. He should've known what you were going to run into. If I were you I'd just forget all about that one as if it'd never happened. Start fresh today.'

He's a good lad, Jim; he bucked me up no end. But O'Neill soon bucked me down again. He was pretty snide about it all and told me I should have assembled all the guests in the front parlour and given them a general dem. But then he patted me on the shoulder and said, 'No, never mind, lad, I was only joking. Don't let it worry you. It takes experience to handle a situation like that. You'll soon learn.'

Which just shows you that people aren't really as bad as they can seem on first impression—are they?

We all went into the sales meeting and this time one of the other fellows did a mock dem with Allen Draper who was so hung-over that he winced every time the needle went through the dem cloth. At last it was all over.

I picked up my leads from O'Neill who gave me a wink and wished me good luck without any snide remarks and then I was walking across to the car all set to go.

'Good luck, Russ,' Jim Stanford called. He stuck his thumb in the air and gave me a wink.

'Thanks, Jim. See you tonight,' I called back.

I started the car and my foot was juddering so much on the accelerator I shot out of the yard in leaps and jerks.

When I cleared town I pulled into the kerb for a minute and had a quiet cigarette and sorted through my leads. They were all fairly close together and in reasonably good districts— which I liked to think had been done purposely by O'Neill to give me a good start. So—I doused the fag and I was off.

The first call was just off Smithdown Road, not far from the park, and the house was in a nice, quiet, respectable-looking street. The houses were all well-painted and had neat curtains on the windows and there were no dirty words chalked on the walls.

As Jim Stanford had taught me, I pulled up a short distance from the house and had a quiet couple of minutes to myself, thinking about the street and the people and how I was going to whip in there and sell a Major. Then, feeling all strong and resolute, I moved on to number twenty-three.

I rang the bell and heard the ding-dong of the chimes in the hall and then I stood there, feeling all weak and irresolute. I had the strongest feeling that the door was going to whip open and there'd be ten thousand people in the hall at a wedding reception, all stewed to the rafters on champagne and ordering six Minors each for cash.

I rang the chimes again.

Or maybe an upper-crust Onslow with a bull-whip in his hand saying, 'Get out of here or I'll peel the skin off your bottom!'

'What do you want?' said the high-key voice in my ear.

I spun round, surprised, because I hadn't heard the door open. And it wasn't open either.

'What do you want, mister?' said the mystery voice.

Two beady blue eyes were putting the triple-whammy on me from the letter-box.

'Hello,' I said, smiling. 'Is your mummy in?'

'No!' the creature snarled.

'Oh!' I said, momentarily stuck for something more potent.

'What do you want?' it said again.

'I've come with the sewing machine, sonny.'

'I'm not a sonny,' it growled. 'I'm a her.'

'Where's your mummy gone?' I said.

It thought for a moment.

'Paris.'

'When will she be back?'

'In a minute.'

The letter-box flap snapped down and I stood confused and dismayed on the doorstep. What to do? The woman surely couldn't have gone far if she'd left the child in the house by itself.

'You can't come in, my mummy says,' said the letter-box.

'When did she say that, sonny?'

'I'm not a sonny, I'm a . . .'

'Yes, sorry, darling.'

'I'm not a darling, either. I'm a girl.'

'What's your name?' I said.

'Andromeda.'

I winced.

'Do they call you An for short?'

'No!' it shouted. 'The whole thing. My mummy says I'm not to let people call me An for short.'

'How old are you, Andromeda?'

'Six. How old are you?'

'Where's your daddy or your granny?'

'How old are you, mister?'

'A hundred and seven. Where's your daddy?'

'He's in jail. Where's yours?'

Oh, this was ridiculous. Why did this never happen to Jim Stanford. He got simple problems like Joe Onslow.

'Where's your daddy?' Andromeda insisted.

'He's in London. He's the king.'

There was a respectful silence. That taught the little monster.

'You're a liar,' she said. 'We haven't got a king—only a queen.'

I walked to the front step and looked up and down the street and even found myself glancing at the sky for flights from Paris.

'Look, darl . . . Andromeda,' I said, getting thoroughly fed up with this, 'your mummy wouldn't leave you alone in the house. Now where is she?'

'In the toilet.'

Now that made sense.

'Well, go and tell her I'm here. Please!'

'Tell her yourself.'

I rang the chimes hard this time and lowered my ear to the letter-box for distant voices. It was a big mistake. Andromeda spat in it.

'You dirty little beast!' I shouted.

I got my hanky out and started wiping the goo away and Andromeda started yowling the house down. Then I heard the footsteps on the stairs and a woman's voice shouting, 'Andromeda, what's the matter, chicken? What's happening down here?'

Andromeda was sobbing her tender little heart out.

'Th ... th ... there's a naughty man out th ... th ... there and he s ... s ... spat at me th ... through the letter-box!'

'Oh, my poor baby ...' clucked mother hen.

The door was yanked open and two fierce eyes glared at me as though I'd just denounced the entire family to the Post Office for not having a telly licence.

'Yes?' she demanded.

I smiled at her and turned on the old charm because that was really the only thing to do.

'Good morning, ma'am,' I drawled. 'I'm afraid there's been a little ... er ... misunderstanding ...'

She was seething. 'Did you spit at my child?'

Oh, my dear uncle Sam! How could anybody believe that a grown man could spit at a child through a letter-box—could they?

I threw up my hands theatrically. 'No ... no, of course not. It was ... well, rather the other way around, as a matter of fact.'

She glared at me, then at her poor baby who was beginning to realize that I was putting my case rather well and was slowly disappearing behind mother's very shapely thighs.

'Do you mean that Andromeda spat at you?' Mum said, unable to believe it.

I was making more of a job with my hanky than was actually necessary, just to stress my point.

'Well, yes ... but I think she was a bit frightened ...'

Andromeda started to emerge from behind the thighs, unable to believe that I was actually defending her. Well, for Pete's

sake, I just had to. Unless I quelled this doo-da right then I
wasn't going to sell a machine to mum in a trillion years.

Mum's expression softened a fraction and she looked down
reproachfully at her offspring.

'Oh, Andromeda, how could you? Now you say you're very,
very sorry to this very nice gentleman.'

Ah ha! Now this was better.

'I'm awfully sorry,' said Mum. 'I was just upstairs ... er ...
making the beds. I do hope she hasn't been too rude to you.
Won't you come in?'

Andromeda shot away down the hall, fearing, possibly, and
with just cause, that I might get a sly punch in if she stayed
too close.

Well, we got settled down quite nicely at a big table in the
living room with Andromeda keeping her distance like the
sweet, intuitive brat that she was, and I went through the dem
on the Minor. Mum bought it like a shot. Loved it! Just the
sort of thing she wanted. I took her money and gave her a
receipt and then she was heading for the kitchen.

'I'm sure you'd love a cup of tea after all your hard work,'
she said over her shoulder. 'Just make yourself comfortable.'

Now was the time to strike, I thought. 'Oh, did you hear our
special offer on commercial radio this morning?' I shouted
through.

She laughed. 'No, what on earth was that?'

'Ha!' I laughed, feeling pretty confident now that the Minor
had gone so well and also feeling that Mum was the sort of
bird you could have a bit of a joke with. She had that sort of
walk, if you know what I mean. I bet she'd been a bit of a flier
before she'd got married and somehow I could tell she still
hadn't quite come in to land. 'You really missed something,' I
said.

'Did I?' she laughed, kind of flirty.

'You certainly did. Just a minute!'

I was down the hallway in a flash and within a couple of
ticks I was back with the Major.

She came in from the kitchen and leaned against the door
post with her nice flat tummy thrust forward and her arms
crossed over her bussoms which were decent handfuls. There
was an intrigued smile dancing around in her eyes.

'What on earth have you got there?' she said, making it
sound as though she was staring at my flies.

Andromeda was picking her nose in the corner.

'Just you wait and see,' I said.

I whipped off the cover and Mum made a funny little groan of delight and pushed herself away from the post with her bottom.

'Oooh!' she went. 'Now that's what I call a machine.'

Andromeda came up and climbed on to a chair, still picking her nose.

'Andromeda, stop that!' commanded Mum.

Andromeda pouted and began scratching her bottom.

'And stop that too!' said Mum.

She smiled an embarrassed apology at me and said, 'Children . . .' and tutted.

'This,' I announced grandly, 'is our very special offer. The fabulous Ritebuy Major.'

Mum got all excited and said, 'Just a minute! I'll pour the tea and then you can show me everything.'

She dashed back into the kitchen and I started getting the machine ready.

'What's that?' said Andromeda, pointing.

'The fly-wheel,' I answered.

'What's it for?'

'Catching flies,' I said.

'And what's that?'

'The foot control.'

'What does that do?'

I sighed. 'It conubulates the frausinskiser assemblage and dinkitorializes the wim-wam.'

'What's a wim-wam?'

Served me right.

'It's for little girls who won't shut up!' I growled. 'It pulls their knickers down and goes WIM-WAM!'

Andromeda backed up about a foot and her lower lip started quivering. I thought for a minute she was going to start bawling again and that would never do, so I decided on diplomacy. I gave her a piece of dem cloth and said, 'Here, make your dolly a dress.'

She took it and said, 'Thank you very much,' and then blew her nose on it. I sneered at her and she sneered right back.

'I don't like your rotten old machine,' she said.

I was going to reply 'and it's not very flamin' keen on you either' but I didn't. I was scared of her. This little horror could massacre this sale if she put her mind to it and it looked very much as if that was exactly what she was doing.

'Don't you want to go and play with your dollies,' I asked sweetly.

'I haven't got any. I've only got guns and a dead beetle.'

'Can I see your guns?'

She thought about it. 'Say please, then.'

'Please, Andromeda?'

'No, you can't!'

Mum came back with two cups of tea in her best china and a plate of chocolate biscuits on a tray.

'Ah, I see you've made friends,' she said. 'There you are, Mr Tobin. Sugar? A biscuit?'

I declined. You can't do a dem with a mouthful of chocolate digestive.

Mum heaved her chair closer to me until her knee was touching mine.

'Sorry,' she said demurely, and moved the knee away but within ten seconds it was back again and I felt a lump like a cricket ball leap into my throat.

'Now, show me your fabulous machine,' she said.

'Can I have a biscuit?' moaned Andromeda.

'No, darling, you've only just had breakfast.'

'Well now, the Ritebuy Major . . .' I started.

'Please, Mummy, can I . . . ?'

'Andromeda darling, I've already told you . . .'

Oh, give the perisher a biscuit, for Chrissake!

'Yeeerrrooowwaaauuuummmmnnoo!' went Andromeda.

'Andromeda! Go to your room at once!'

Silence.

'Well, then, just one,' said Mum, 'but mind you eat your lunch.'

'Now, this machine . . .'

'Can I have two?'

'ONE!'

'Beetle wants one.'

'Beetle's dead. Besides, beetles don't eat chocolate biscuits.'

'What do they eat?'

I began wondering what they were doing in nice, sane, boring old Wainwrights at that moment. Sitting in absolute, beautiful silence, scratching away at the ledgers . . .

'I'm so sorry, Mr Tobin, you were saying . . . ?'

'I want to wee-wee.'

'Well go and do it, darling, you can do it by yourself.'

'Don't want to now.'

'Well, what did you say you did for?'

' 'Cos I felt like it then but I don't now.'

Mum closed her eyes and sighed to me. 'I'm sorry, Mr Tobin . . .'

Andromeda actually shut up for about fifteen seconds, apart from a slight choking fit when she got some crumbs in her throat, and I managed to get the facts of the special offer over to Mum. And all the time I was talking to her there was that secret smile going on in her eyes like it was all just one big sexy secret between the two of us. What we were doing, of course, was screwing each other optically and she was enjoying it no end.

Her knee would flick out every now and again and just touch mine and then she would draw it back and maybe cross her legs, pretending to get the offending member out of the way, but in fact showing me what delicious thighs she had.

I don't really know what I was talking about half the time because Prince Richard was doing his level best to fracture my ribs and my head was going round like Earlybird.

Anyway, I got the dem going and she sat there fascinated and I thought this is a cinch. No woman could have been more interested in either the machine or the salesman and when you get that sort of combination running for you, you've got yourself a sale! Well, we were toddling along fine. I'd sewed backwards and forwards and she'd said, 'Oh, can I try that?' and she'd come round and put her hand on mine while I was flicking the lever up and down and trying to ignore her charlies that were sticking deliciously into the back of my neck. Then I'd shown her the attachments and got through those nicely and I was just coming up to the closing pitch when it happened. That damned child got her hand caught in the flywheel!

She climbed on to the table and simply pushed her grubby little mitt through one of the holes while the wheel was stationary and there it was—stuck.

Well, she let out a yowl that the lads in the docks must have thought was their tiffin whistle and Mum started flying around in ever-increasing circles threatening to call the police and the fire brigade and the Women's Institute and the Cats' Home and I was flying around after her trying to calm her down and shut the kid up at the same time.

'Have you got any Vaseline?' I said, and she gave me a very funny look. Then it registered that I wasn't proposing anything indecent and she dashed off to the bathroom.

'There, you see,' I said to Dracula's daughter, 'that's what you get for interfering.'

'It was your stupid machine,' she said between sniffs. 'Mummy doesn't want your rotten machine. It stinks!'

I looked longingly at the foot control and for a split second . . .

Mum came hurtling down the stairs and nearly fractured herself on the rug at the bottom.

'Oh, my poor baby . . .' she was moaning.

I plastered the kid's hand with Vaseline and began easing it back through the hole. Mum stood by, wringing her hands and cooing and tutting all over the place. Finally it popped out and we all gave a big sigh of relief. Now, perhaps, I could get back to selling the flaming thing.

'I don't like that naughty machine, Mummy. Tell him to take it away.'

Mum looked sadly at me and longingly at the Major.

'Oh, it isn't really a naughty machine, darling. You shouldn't have put your hand in it.'

Andromeda started bawling again and I could see my first sale flying out of the window.

'It really is a wonderful buy, madam,' I insisted, trying to get the advantage back in my corner. 'Let me tell you about . . .'

Mum was shaking her head.

'I'm a little upset at the moment, Mr Tobin. She gave me a terrible fright. Could you come back in, say, half an hour and perhaps we can carry on? I do like it very much but baby's in such a state and I think I ought to try to settle her down.'

Baby looked perfectly marvellous. She was peeping from behind the thighs again and daring me to contradict Mum.

I retired gracefully and smoked two cigarettes in the car and my spirits were sinking lower with every drag. Well, that was it, I just knew. Andromeda would start working on Mumsy and I'd be lucky if she even spoke to me, never mind buy the machine when I went back. No, it wasn't just defeatist thinking, it was a very real premonition.

Women . . . kids . . . ! Oh, I was feeling bitter.

I gave her an extra three minutes over the half hour and then dejectedly rang the door chimes again. Mum opened the door and, so help me, she was smiling at me, all flirty again!

'Come in, Mr Tobin. I'm so sorry about all that. Andromeda's much better now.'

We went into the living room and blind me if the little perisher wasn't sitting at the table fiddling with doll's dresses.

'We've had a long talk,' said Mum, 'and I've told Andromeda that if we buy the machine we can make new clothes for all her dollies—so she'd like us to have it.'

I stared at her.

'But . . . I thought she didn't have any dolls,' I said.

Andromeda spun round in her chair.

' 'Course I have, stupid. All girls have dolls, don't they?'

Well, nothing could stop me now—I was away! It was as easy as that. Mind you, I didn't sell any more that day—and yet I did, if you know what I mean. Because when I got back to the shop that night, Allen Draper, who was looking so much better by then, came smiling up to me and said, 'Congratulations, Russ, you've sold a machine!'

I was a bit shaken by this.

'How do you know?' I said.

Then he looked a bit puzzled.

'Did you sell one of your leads today?' he asked.

'Yes,' I said.

'Good boy, then you've sold two today!'

'Eh?'

'Yes, a Mr . . . er . . . Whatshisname . . . Renowski came into the shop and brought your Minor back . . . said his daughter didn't want such a small one and could he see the Special Offer you'd been telling him about. So I just showed him the Major and he bought it—so the sale goes down to you.'

Well, you could've knocked me over. That wedding reception hadn't turned out badly at all, had it? Selling a Major *and* getting a fair old piece of the other from that darling little pigeon Samantha. And that was ten quid I'd earned for Monday! Nearly two-thirds of what I got for a whole week's slog down at Wainwright's. Now, if I could just do that every day . . . !

Tuesday was a bad day—I didn't sell a sausage. Two of my four leads were out all day and I couldn't even sell the Minor to the other two!

Funny women, they were. One of them had just had her cat run over and was in mourning, so to speak. So to speak!—she had the coffin lying in state in the front room and she took the lid off and made me look at the wretched animal—all stiff and glassy-eyed, it was, because the bloke who was to prepare it properly hadn't turned up yet. Quite put me off my lunch. Still, I could sense her grief and got out of there fast and promised to come back in a week's time.

The fourth woman must have been having it off with her boy-friend when I rang the bell. She came to the door in a yellow dressing gown with her hair all over the place and her lipstick up her nose practically.

She invited me in and listened politely enough but I could tell from the way she kept looking at the ceiling that she'd got her second wind and was figuring that the boy-friend had too. So I got out of there, too. Well, you're just wasting your time trying to compete with a fellow in bed, aren't you? Upstairs she was getting all the needle she wanted for a bit without bothering about mine, if you'll pardon the joke.

They didn't say anything down at Ritebuy about me having a bad day, just said it happened to everybody at some time or other and left it at that. Actually, I think they'd decided to let me have my first week to myself without comment and see how I shaped up. Which was very sensible of them too because I felt better when I started out on Wednesday for not getting a bollocking on Tuesday.

Wednesday, now there was a day to remember!

ELEVEN

Wednesday.

I muffed the first sale badly and had a terrible fight trying to kill the Minor sale—all of which upset me for the day. I was shaking all over when I got back to the car because the husband had been very nasty and had made outright accusations that both the company and I were crooked and reckoned he was going to expose us to the Chamber of Commerce and the Better Business Bureau and God only knows who else. Nasty type, he was. I felt like sewing the end of his thing up.

And so I wasn't feeling too confident when I knocked at the big house near Stanley Park.

A nice old man answered the door and his smile put me at ease a bit and I went in to meet his wife, who was also nice-looking. Mr and Mrs Ainsworth, they were.

Well, after a cup of tea and a chat I waltzed through the Minor dem but I could feel the old boy wasn't very impressed with the looks of the Minor and I thought this was going to be another abort.

And then he said, 'Er ... Mr Tobin, please don't think me rude, but I do feel my dear wife would appreciate something a little more ... er ... shall we say, substantial. Do you have anything of that nature?'

'Substantial?' I said, hoping that he was meaning what I was hoping he was meaning.

'Yes,' he said, 'Er ... something a little more expensive.'

Did I? I shattered all records from the house to the car and back again and set up the Major on the table. Then I whipped off the cover like a head chef revealing some culinary miracle and stood back.

'Ah!' they both said and gave each other little looks.

'Now, this is more like it,' said the old man. 'What do you think, dear?'

'It's beautiful, dear.'

'Er ... how much is it, Mr Tobin?' asked Mr Ainsworth.

'Er ...'

Now this was tricky—because we could really charge what we liked for the Major if the opportunity ever presented itself —as it was obviously doing now. There was no standard retail price, see, because it was only Ritebuy that sold the Major. And if we sold it for more than fifty pounds we got half the difference in commission!

'Seventy pounds,' I said nonchalantly.

All right, I knew it was a bit steep but I could always come down on the Special Offer if they objected—but it meant an extra *ten* quid in commission and the old folk didn't look pushed for a bob or two.

'Yes, exactly,' the old man was saying. 'Stands out a mile that it's superior to this little fellow.' He waved his hand at the Minor which had faded into insignificance in the shadow of the Major. He turned almost coyly to his wife and winked at her.

'Would you like it, dearest?'

'Oh, Henry, I would love it!'

Poor souls, they looked so sweet and nice I just couldn't diddle them, even for an extra tenner.

'Ah, but I have a surprise for you,' I heard myself saying. 'Today, this machine is on Special Offer at not seventy pounds ... not even sixty pounds...' well, if I was going to be a sucker I may as well do it with a bit of style, '... but at only forty-nine pounds ten shillings!'

They both gasped a bit and the old man said, 'There, my dear, now we certainly must have it. Right, Mr Tobin, you have a sale. Will a cheque be all right?'

My word, would it?

Well, I got down to work and I was showing Mrs Ainsworth how to work the attachments and things when the front door bell went.

'I'll get it,' said the old man who'd been standing watching us.

I could hear him greet somebody in the hallway and then he came back with a middle-aged woman.

'... it really is a beautiful machine,' he was saying to her. 'Er ... this is our daughter, Mr Tobin—Mrs Radock.'

I got up and said how d'you do and Mrs Radock joined the sewing circle and started rabbiting to her mum about it all.

She was really impressed, the daughter.

'Oh, I must try and get a new one,' she said miserably. 'Really, that old hand-machine of mine drives me mad. Oh, do let me have a go, Mum, can I?'

Well, she got down to it and started ripping up the track—backwards and forwards and round in circles and the two of them were laughing their heads off like a couple of mattress stuffers in a feather factory.

'Oh, it's gorgeous!' the daughter kept saying.

Then the old man winked at me and my tum flipped over because I could sense what he was going to say.

'Would you like one, darling?' he said quietly.

There was a deathly silence and you could see she was knocked for six.

'Oh, Dad, I couldn't ...' she said sorrowfully. 'You've been so good to us already ...'

'Well, what's the stuff for but to spend?' he said, waving his hand in the air. 'That's why we tried to win it in the first place, wasn't it?'

What was all this?

'Yes, I know ...' said the daughter reluctantly.

'Well then, you shall have one,' said her dad. 'Mr Tobin, could you deliver one down the road to my daughter's place?'

'Yes, sir!' I said, trying hard not to kiss him. 'I've got another one in the car.'

Well, now, you might be thinking that this sounds like a bit of a fairy tale and that folks who do their own sewing just haven't got that sort of money to fling about. But it's quite true and I think you might have guessed how the old boy could do it.

As I was leaving with the daughter he went to the sideboard and brought out a slip of paper and handed it to me.

'I'd just like to show you this,' he said nicely, not showing off or anything. 'You look like a young fellow that can appreciate a bit of fun and I'd like you to see what has brought an awful lot of fun into our old lives.' He gave a little laugh. 'It also sold you two machines today, Mr Tobin—so perhaps you'll have a bit of fun on the commission!'

I looked at the slip of paper. It was a cancelled cheque that had been presented by Littlewoods Pools to Mr H. Ainsworth.

It was for seventy-eight thousand four hundred and seventeen pounds, eighteen shillings and fourpence.

Everything else that was to happen that week must, I thought, be one howling anti-climax. And indeed it was—until Friday afternoon.

I was then coasting along with a comfortable eight sales in the bag and forty glorious quid in my pocket and I felt like King Dick himself (who, incidentally, is no relation to Prince Richard).

At lunch time on Friday I sat in a slightly better class of transport cafe than I usually frequented and thought about the coming week-end. It had to be something really special in celebration of a great first week at Ritebuy and must, necessarily, include the fair sex. Who was the lucky little darling going to be? Gloria? Samantha? The Countess of Bootle?

I had another egg sandwich and thought it over. I put aside the 'who' for a moment and concentrated on the 'what'. What could I do that was really exciting and different—bearing in mind that I intended to blow the entire forty quid in one stupendous once-in-a-lifetime orgy? Oh, the power of real money! How about a cruise? Jamaica! The Bahamas!

I thought about that cheque for seventy-eight thousand quid. Seventy ... eight ... thousand ... quid. Didn't matter how you said it—fast or slow—it was a terrible lot of money. You could buy ... what could you buy with seventy-eight thousand quid? I got my pencil out and started doing some calculations on the menu.

3,120,000 packets of chewing gum at 6*d*. per.

78 Vauxhall Crestas—with a bit over for petrol.

312,000 egg and chips at 5*s*. (How many chips?)

857 years of going to the pictures 7 nights a week at 5*s*.

428 years 6 months of ditto if you take a bird and pay for her.

520,000 packets of Durex at 3*s*. per pack. (!)

'D'you mind!' said the waitress, whipping the menu away. 'Other people have got to read it too, you know.'

She had hairy legs and a funny eye—ergo her bad temper. Q.E.D.

What was I going to do?

At two o'clock I still hadn't worked it out so I let it ride. Something would come to me, no doubt.

I checked my last call for the day. It was a Mrs Standish, Flat 12, Branston Mansions, Knotty Ash. Well, Mrs Standish, stand by for Ritebuy's super salesman!

I left the waitress sixpence because of her funny eye and departed.

It was a super day—a little touch of spring fanning the air and getting everybody excited about another miserable summer. I wound the windows down and sang all the way to Knotty Ash.

My word, now Branston Mansions was quite something.

There was an air of quiet presumed wealth hanging around the place like a thick morning mist. You could see it half a block away. No rubbish here.

I pushed through the double doors and walked up one flight of stairs on carpet thick enough to lose a tortoise in. At number twelve I pushed the bell and got chimes again, but this time very dulcet and very expensive ones. The corridor smelt good, as if the management had sprayed it with French perfume. It tickled my sense and made me think of Samantha. 'I looove you, Samanthaaa,' I sang to myself.

The door opened and Mrs Standish stood tnere and, believe me, I forgot all about Samantha just like that. This was the most edible piece of pulchritude I'd ever been this close to. She was about twenty-five—give or take a hangover—fair to middling tall and she had all her protuberances and concavities in exactly the right locations. She was wearing a pair of white cotton trousers that were so tight I could see the outline of a mole on her right thigh and a blue sweater that must have jumped for joy when she bought it. She smiled at me slowly through a piece of her blonde, blonde hair and I just knew we were going to be very good friends.

'Hi!' she said, massaging me from head to knees with the little word.

'Mrs Standish?' I said.

'No,' she said, 'I'll get her,' and backed into the apartment.

Ah, well.

But wait a minute—we live again. Her mate was almost the spitting image of her only she had brown hair and yellow pants and a white sweater.

'Hello,' she said.

A bit more formal, you see, and I quite like a bit of reserve to start off with.

'Mrs Standish,' I said again, and if she'd said 'No, I'll go and get her' I would have run screaming out of the building.

'Yes,' she said.

I told her who I was and she stood aside to let me pass.

It was like walking into the perfume counter at Lewis's. Oh, it smelled delicious—not cheap mind you, no, really subtle stuff that crept up your back and undid your braces. And the flat! There must have been two hundred quid's worth of sofa sitting on the Chinese rug and everything else was likewise.

Blondie was sitting on the sofa by now with her legs curled up under her bum and she was just about to light a fag about

116

two feet long.

'This is my friend, Mrs Van Huys,' said Mrs Standish. 'She lives just down the hall.'

I'll bet she does, I thought. What in blazes do chicks like this want with a sewing machine?

'Hi again,' said Blondie, giving me an encore of the smile through the hair. Very effective, that, if it's done properly.

'I must go, angel,' she said to Mrs Standish. She got up off the sofa like a white and blue panther and padded across to the door. I got the wake of her perfume as she passed me and I went all funny in the head.

'See you later, honey,' she said, opening the door, and I damn-near said, 'O.K., baby.'

She went out and Mrs Standish gave me a funny sort of look and waved me to the sofa.

'She's beautiful, isn't she?' she said.

'Hm? Oh, er . . . yes . . .'

'More beautiful than I?'

I thought something had gone wrong with my ears. I gaped at her.

'Well . . .?' she said.

'Er . . . no . . .'

'What's your name?'

'Tobin.'

'Your first name. I know it's Tobin, you told me.'

'Russell . . . er . . . Russ.'

She smiled at me, just like Blondie had done it.

'That's nice.'

She looked at me for about ten seconds and I just knew that all my clothes were lying in a big heap on the floor.

'What have you got for me, Russ?'

'Mm?'

'The machine. Isn't that a machine?'

'Oh . . . yes . . . er . . . have you got a larger table than this?' I pointed to the little glass-topped coffee table in front of us.

She flicked her eyes towards a little dining alcove across the room that I hadn't even noticed up to now and I made a move to get up. She smiled and put her hand out to stop me.

'There's plenty of time for that. Would you like a drink?'

Without waiting for an answer she spun off the sofa and went to a trolley by the wall that was loaded with glasses and bottles of all sorts of hootch. And then, suddenly, I realized that she was just a teensy bit tipsy. She and her pal had been on a lunchtime session when I'd walked in. They weren't drunk, mind you, far from it, but this one was definitely quite mellow and thinking back Blondie must have been too.

'Vodka?' she said.

Ah, that was the answer! No smell, see.

'Thank you, just a small one . . .'

She came over to me with about thirty-two fingers of neat Vodka in two very tall glasses and a bottle of bitter lemon tucked under her arm. She put the glasses on the coffee table and said, 'Say when,' and tipped in a gesture of bitter lemon.

'To you, Russ Tobin,' she said, looking at me over the top of her glass.

'To you, Mrs Standish.'

What the hell . . . it was Friday and it was my last call . . .

'Helen,' she said.

'To you, Helen.'

'To us, Russ.'

We examined each other's eyeballs while we drank some Vodka. Oh, it's pernicious stuff, Vodka—sneaky, no smell. Not much taste, either and no kick apparently—not until it reaches your lower ribs . . .

'Tell me about you, Russ,' she said.

She offered me a cigarette box from the table and took one herself, then she held my hand steady while I touched a flame to her fag. I was shaking like a table jelly.

'What about?'

She looked up from the flame.

'All about. Where did you go for your holiday last year?'

What a funny lady!

'I didn't have one.'

'I did,' she said.

'Oh, where did you go?'

'Camping.'

'Oh?'

'I've got some photographs. Would you like to see them?'

'Yes.'

She floated away to a long, low sideboard and took a pack of photographs from the drawer. Then she floated back again, only this time she practically sat on my knee when she settled down. She handed me a photo snap and I could hardly bring myself to look at it.

It was a scene of rural beauty. A line of green hills set above a shimmering blue lake.

118

'Windermere,' she said.

'It's beautiful.'

She handed me the second one. This was a closer shot of the hill and now there was a big blue tent pegged out in the field below it. There was quite a bit of camping equipment arranged in front of the tent—primus stove, barbeque stand, chairs, air mattresses . . .

'Nice,' I said.

'Beautiful tent,' she said in my ear. 'Very comfortable.'

Next one. This was the same shot but now standing by the tent was a man. He looked stern, tanned, pot-bellied and in his mid-fifties. Typical executive type—grey-haired, distinguished.

'My husband,' she said casually. 'He's . . . a little older than I.'

She leaned forward for her drink and quite accidentally massaged my knee-cap with her breast.

'Drink up,' she said and we toasted each other in silence.

'This one's of me,' she said. 'It was very hot up there.'

Again the tent but this time Helen had replaced her old man. I nearly dropped the photograph. Apart from a small leaf which she was holding jokingly in front of her she was starkers. I gulped and reached for my Vodka.

Helen chuckled about an eighth of an inch from my ear. 'Charles thought that one up. He calls it "Eve'll in tent." Rather good, isn't it? Do you like it, Russ?'

I made a funny noise.

'Do you think I'm beautiful, Russ,' she murmured, and I could hear excitement trembling in her voice.

'Yes . . . very . . .'

'Here's another one of me.'

This one was taken much, much closer and must have been shot in autumn. She was just plain starkers. She was lying on a multi-coloured air-bed and smiling up at the camera.

'Kiss me,' she said, just quietly in my ear.

I turned my head slowly and fell down a long, warm tunnel into a frenzy of blatant frustration. We rugby-scrummed for a few minutes and then she pushed me gently away, slipped off the sofa and crossed to the door, straightening her clothes. For a weird moment I thought I was going to get the boot—until I heard the double lock click on the door. She turned and wandered back to me, her eyes all dreamy and languid. She knelt down by the coffee table and handed me my drink and then lazily tipped hers to her lips.

'Busy this afternoon?' she murmured into her glass.

I shook my head. 'This is my last call.'

She smiled at the rim of her glass and got up quickly, as though she'd suddenly reached a decision. She wandered away down a small hallway towards where the bedroom must have been, but she didn't go into the bedroom. In a second or two I heard the shower turned on and the curtain pulled across.

'Russ . . .' she called.

I took a gulp of Vodka and got up off the sofa, knowing that the whole thing was a dream and that any minute Mickey Mouse would start ringing his bells and spoil the whole thing . . .

I stood in the bathroom door and watched the steam rising from behind the black and white curtain. On a chair by the bath were a pair of yellow cotton pants, a white sweater, a bra and a pair of dainty yellow nylon panties.

'I'm having trouble soaping my back,' she called. 'Do you think you could possibly . . .'

Honi soi qui mal y pense. Eve'll be to him who evil thinks.

About four o'clock she rolled over me and flicked the end of my nose with her long fingernails.

'You *are* a big boy, aren't you,' she murmured, her eyes lazy and teasing. 'You must drink an awful lot of milk.'

She wriggled all over me, as if she couldn't get close enough, and I felt a shiver run right through her slim, solid body. I also felt something else happening.

'And getting bigger all the time . . .' she murmured. Suddenly she straddled me and flung herself upright, throwing her head up at the ceiling and sucking in her breath between her teeth and closing her eyes tight.

'Ooooohhh!' she gasped and I grinned up at her, feeling the excitement that comes to a man when he's really driving a woman round the bend.

'Oooohhh, Russell Tobin . . . !'

Then she was leaping up and down like Horsefly Henderson coming round Tattenham Corner and she let out a yell that must have frightened the seagulls off the Liver Buildings.

'Ooohh, you beautiful, gorgeous, king-size man, you,' she groaned and collapsed in a gasping heap all over me.

I was killing myself laughing.

'Huuuuuhh, huuuhh,' she went, trying to get her breath back and kissing me wildly all over the chest and neck and face at the same time. Gradually she subsided and then she sat up again and looked down at me with a look of sheer incredulity which quickly changed to one of shock.

'Oh oh!' she laughed and shot off to the bathroom.

She came back with a hand towel which she slung at me and then jumped back into bed and cuddled up tight. For a minute we just lay there and listened to our breathing gradually returning to sanity.

'Are you married?' she said suddenly.

I shook my head.

'You should be,' she said. 'You're being extremely cruel to some poor girl.'

I chuckled at her.

'Why did you get married?' I asked.

She shrugged and suddenly looked serious. 'Security.' There was a pause, then she said, 'It's a terrible mistake, isn't it?'

I shrugged. 'I wouldn't know. Doesn't he make love to you?'

She laughed unhumorously.

'He's never home. He's in the Argentine right now. I haven't seen him for three months.'

'What does he do?' I asked.

'Engineering. He builds bridges and things in Godforsaken places.'

'Couldn't you go with him?'

She shook her head. 'No, company rules. It's too dangerous.' She slipped her hand on to my chest and tickled my nipple. 'You don't know just what you've done for me today, Russell Tobin. I was going mad for a man.'

I slipped my arm around her and kissed her lightly on the eye. 'I'm mighty glad I was on the spot. I should hate to think of all that going somewhere else.'

'There's a lot more where that came from,' she said seriously. 'No, I'm not a nympho—just human and a bit hot-blooded—like you.'

I squeezed her and laughed. 'You've got me taped.'

'And why shouldn't we be?' she said adamantly. 'A lot of people think that being sexy is akin to being insane or something.. We're a cold-blooded race, aren't we?'

'It's the weather,' I said.

'Well, screw them,' she said. 'If I want a man I'm going to have a man ...' her hand shot down and grabbed me, '... and preferably this one.'

121

I laughed and pressed her to me and then we just lay there in silence for a moment.

Suddenly she raised her head and looked at me with mock puzzlement.

'By the way, why did you come here?'

I laughed at her. 'To flog you a very expensive sewing machine.'

She frowned. 'I wouldn't call five pounds very expensive.'

'Oh, that was only the come-on. I've got a much better machine in the car. I was going to try to sell you that.'

'How much is that?' she said.

'Fifty quid.'

'What!'

'Yes, fifty quid.'

'Huh, how on earth did you propose getting fifty pounds out of me?'

'Well, it's like this . . .'

And, strange though it may seem, there was I lying in bed with my prospective customer, giving her a big cuddle while she was playing around with anything that caught her fancy, and giving her a machine-less dem of the Major.

When I'd finished, she said, 'And do you sell many that way?'

'Millions.'

She sighed like she was giving in after a long struggle. 'Well, I suppose I'd better have one then.'

I looked at her, surprised. 'D'you mean it?'

She nodded reluctantly and sighed again and then she grinned at me and flung herself at me.

'Of course I'll have one, but only if . . .'

I looked at her with suspicion. 'Yes, madam?'

'Only if you promise to come back and demonstrate it properly.'

'Certainly, madam. Shall I put you down for a regular weekly service too?'

'You can service me every day if you want to,' she murmured. 'All day and every day,' and I felt her breath go as sweet as a nut and her heart start banging like a bongo. And then, once again, she was riding a cockhorse to Banbury Cross as if the hound of the Baskerville was after her. Full pelt down the straight she went, whooping it up with the wind screaming through her hair and her mouth wide open in some private, screaming frenzy.

'Whhhooooo!' she went as she took the last hurdle and landed smack in Beecher's Brook. 'Oooh, you beautiful, beautiful sewing machine man!'

After she'd weighed in and been declared winner, I said, 'I must go.'

She moaned pitifully. 'Must you? Can't you stay all night? I'll make you a lovely dinner...'

I shook my head and kissed her. 'I'm a working man. I must report in to H.Q.'

All of which wasn't strictly true, because, provided we had enough machines for the following day, we were allowed to phone in for our leads instead of dragging all the way into town and all the way out again. But somehow I felt that it'd been so good between us that we might just knock the edge off if I stayed too long—you know, a little and often being much more durable than making a pig of yourself with one mighty thrash.

So, reluctantly, she let me get out of bed and we had a nice platonic shower together and then I went down to the car and brought the Major up.

'Oh, it's lovely,' she said, without too much enthusiasm. 'Yes, I'll have it, Russ.'

I looked at her seriously. 'Are you sure, now? I don't want you to think that just because ... you know ...'

She laughed and shook her head. 'No, I'm not doing you any favour.'

'What on earth do you want a sewing machine for, anyway?' I said, looking around the opulent apartment.

She shrugged. 'Oh, it's just an idea. Chris and I thought we might take up dressmaking—to relieve the boredom.'

'Chris?'

'Yes, you met her. She opened the door for you.'

'Oh ... yes.'

So Blondie might be in the market for a machine, too!

'Does she want a machine?' I asked with painful nonchalance.

It didn't fool Helen one bit. She gave me a very old-fashioned look.

'Possibly ...' she drawled, '... but that's all you're going to sell her, my sweet ram.'

I conjured up a look of innocence that was worth an M.G.M. contract any day of the week.

'... and when you give her a demonstration, *I'm* going to be present.'

I tried to laugh. 'Good Lord . . .'

'She's as frustrated as I am,' she said with disgust. 'Her husband sleeps in a jet for nine months of the year. He calls her twice a week from Honolulu, New York, Afghanistan, Wogga Wogga . . .'

'Bring her in then,' I said. 'I'll do a dem for both of you.'

She launched herself at me and gave me a big hug.

'Oh, I didn't mean it. You can screw her too, if you want to.'

I tried to look suitably hurt. 'Oh, no . . . for Pete's sake, you don't think I go around seducing women into buying . . .'

She shook her head and crossed to the door, laughing. 'No, I don't. But I do think there's an awful lot of women that'd love to seduce you into selling. I won't be a minute.'

She disappeared out of the door and I started getting the Major fixed up on the table. I'd just finished when I heard them chatting in the hallway and then Blondie was coming into the room and giving me a very meaningful look. She knew, of course, what had been going on by the amount of time I'd been in the flat and there was excitement in her soulful blue eyes as she smiled at me.

Helen followed her in, looking a little bit self-conscious but mostly just smug. They came over to the table and Chris's perfume started running up my back and stoking my boilers again. She came very close and peeped round my shoulder.

'Helen tells me you might be interested in a machine,' I said to her.

Her eyes flicked up to mine and a mischievous grin started pecking at her moist red lips.

'Yes . . . I might,' she said slowly.

'Well . . .' I had to cough to clear my throat. 'Well, I'd like to show you how it works.'

I ran through the dem quickly, conscious all the time of the silent intrigue that was going on between the three of us. I don't think any one of us gave a hoot about what I was saying.

'So there you are, ladies . . . that's the famous Ritebuy Major.'

'What d'you think, Chris?' Helen asked.

I turned round to look up at Chris and her eyes swept slowly across mine on their way to the machine.

'I'd love it,' she said, suggestively. 'When can you deliver, Mr Tobin?'

'Right away. I've got another in the car.'

'So bring it up!' she laughed.

I just couldn't believe it—TEN machines in my first week and still Saturday morning to go! I went down to the car in a bit of a haze.

At the car I checked the time. It was half past six. Did I want to spend the night with Helen? I'd have to go home sometime and get some clean clothes and have a shave. Maybe I could nip home now and then come back? I really didn't know if I wanted to.

I lugged the Major out of the car and stumbled up the stairs. I was beginning to feel a bit weak in the knees.

Chris was waiting outside Helen's closed door when I got back and Helen must have been inside.

'You look all in, Russ,' she said meaningfully and smiled as she turned away down the hall. 'Down here.'

She opened the door with a key and went in, holding the door open for me.

Her flat was just as grand as Helen's and warm with magnificent greens and blues and oranges. Funny, isn't it? All that comfort and luxury and they were still two bored, frustrated women, so lonely despite all that money that they were thinking of taking up dressmaking to pass the time away. They're right, you know—the blokes who preach that without love and companionship nothing counts in this sweet life. These chickens would have been as interested in me as I am for our milkman if their husbands had spent more time at home instead of gallivanting around all over the globe. Or would they? I don't know.

'Over there, if you please, Mr Tobin,' she said.

I watched the trim white pants lead away across the lounge to a little table by the wall. I put the Major down gently and felt her come close to me.

'I feel cheated,' she pouted.

'Oh?'

'Yes ... it took you four whole hours to convince Helen that she ought to buy your machine and you've spent exactly five minutes on me.'

I coughed.

'Now, d'you think that's fair?'

I laughed. 'No ... I suppose ...'

'And on second thoughts, Mr Tobin, I'm not sure now that I'm going to buy it. I think I've rushed into it far too quickly and I think I'm going to take a lot of convincing before I write out that cheque.'

'Well . . . it's a bit difficult, isn't it? I mean . . .'

I looked nervously at the door, which was still open, expecting Helen to be standing there.

'Because of Helen?' she asked.

I nodded and she shook her head slowly and smiled at me.

'Helen won't mind, Mr Tobin—I'm her best friend.'

She crossed to the door and closed it slowly and meticulously, as if savouring every portion of the act, and then she turned and leaned against it and looked at me.

'You . . .' she said quietly, '. . . and I . . .' she came back across the deep carpet and stood before me, looking up into my face, her own quite serious, '. . . are going to have a good . . . long . . .', her arms came up behind my neck and she slowly drew my mouth down to hers, '. . . chat!'

'Oh, just a little higher, darling,' she moaned. 'Up on the shoulder blade.'

I ran the softly humming massager up her straight white spine and floated it on to her shoulder. She squirmed deliciously into the rose-coloured silk counterpane and moaned softly.

'That . . . is . . . heaven,' she murmured. 'Mmmmmmmm.'

I brought the buzzing titillator down again, running it straight down her spine. A shudder ran through her and goose pimples shot up like coarse sandpaper all over her body.

'Oh!' she laughed. 'Oh, Russ, don't . . . don't stop!'

'Turn over.'

She giggled and flipped over and I started drawing small circles on her hard, flat tum. Then the circles got bigger . . .

She brought her knees up and laughed aloud. 'Careful . . . careful . . . !'

I had to laugh because she was giggling so much. She brought her legs down again and I took the machine right down to her toes and very gently started working my way up. By the time I got to her thigh she was in hysterics.

'Oh, let me do you,' she gasped and shot up on the bed. So I handed her the machine and stretched out on my tum.

It really was incredible. I'd never been vibro-ed before and as soon as she started I knew what I'd been missing. All the tension and tiredness seemed to float away—sucked out by the little pulsating rubber pad.

126

'Oh, brother . . .'

'You like?' she laughed.

Up and down . . . around and around . . .

'Now you turn over,' she giggled.

'Go easy, we fellows are built differently to you ladies.'

'Oh?'

She had me so ticklish I couldn't breathe properly. I was doubled up and rolling off the bed, gasping, 'No . . . now stop it . . . that's enough!'

She clicked off the machine and lay down by me and stroked my face until we'd calmed down a bit.

'You're a lot of fun,' she said softly. 'A whole lot.'

I kissed her on the nose. 'So are you.'

She sighed and looked up at the ceiling. 'Do you . . . do you have a thumping big conscience.'

I looked at her. 'What, about Helen and you?'

She nodded.

'No, not at all.'

And that was the truth. Somehow it hadn't been pure lechery . . . oh, well, I suppose it had really, but it certainly hadn't felt like it. It had all been good clean stuff and the fact that I was lying there feeling so relaxed and not wanting to dash down to the car and get a billion miles away from Branston Mansions was the proof of it as far as I was concerned. And that's the yardstick in my book. If you can feel happy with another human being after a relationship, and you haven't hurt anybody else in the process, then it must have been worthwhile. Of course it might be considered that we'd hurt the absent husbands and everyone's entitled to his own opinion but I didn't see it quite that way. I didn't have to try very hard to believe that I'd actually done those two fellows a favour. They were going to come back home from their travels to find two satisfied, happy wives instead of a couple of frustrated grumps.

I actually began to feel quite public-spirited.

'Neither do I,' Chris said. 'Does that sound awful?'

I shook my head. 'Not to me, darlin'. It might to some, but then, they don't know all the facts, do they?'

She looked at me very nicely. 'Will you come and see me again?'

'Most assuredly.'

She hesitated. 'And Helen?'

I hesitated. 'Well, I did promise . . .'

She snuggled up, very pleased. 'Good, I wouldn't want to monopolize you. After all, she did send in the coupon.'

I laughed at her. 'You really are good mates, aren't you? All for one and one for all. But . . . er . . .'

'Yes, darling?'

'Could we make it on separate days?' I said. 'I'm buggered.'

TWELVE

Now, I don't want to give the impression that every week was like that first week, with me selling ten machines and laying forty-seven beautiful women in sumptuous apartments. Nothing could be further from the truth. Actually, after that, it was more like eight machines and twenty-three beautiful women in sumptuous apartments! No, but seriously, there were some pretty bad weeks to follow and I must tell you an amusing thing that happened at the end of one of those weeks that sort of gave me one back at Tom O'Neill who was still being a bit officious and nasty. In fact I think it was the turning point in our relationship because after what happened he became much more reasonable.

Well, I'd been there about two months and over all things hadn't been too bad. I'd had one glorious week with fourteen sales when everything had gone just perfect but then I'd had a couple of rotten ones with only five and four sales respectively, and by the Friday of the third week I'd only done four again.

I was feeling a bit down in the mouth when O'Neill beckoned me into the sales room and closed the door.

'Sit down, son,' he said ominously.

Well, that got right up my jacket for a start because I do hate being called son.

He turned his chair round and straddled it and sat shaking his head at me like I'd just wet my pants or something.

'Now, what's the trouble, son?' he said.

I shrugged at him. 'Just a bad patch.'

'It's a three-week bad patch, isn't it?' he said quietly. 'And none of the other fellows are in it.'

This wasn't strictly true because two or three of the lads had been moaning about sales lately. They reckoned it was the sudden flush of hot weather which, unbelievably, had come to our green and soggy little island. However, they had done better than muggins here.

'Perhaps you're a little stale,' O'Neill suggested, making it sound like I wanted a bath.

'I don't think so . . .'

'Ah, but very often the salesman can't tell. Sometimes you're stale without knowing it. It takes an independent witness to spot it.'

I just knew what was coming and I shuddered.

'So I think I'll come out with you today and see if I can't straighten things out.'

Well, that did put the mockers on it. If I was going stale by myself I'd be rock-banging rotten with old Copper Nob breathing down my neck. Anway I couldn't argue, so I just set my mind to disaster and got on with it.

Driving through town he got quite chatty.

'You mustn't let this little hiatus worry you, son. It happens to all of us at some time or other—mind that bus, won't you? I myself, when I was on the road, had some bad weeks. Mind you, that was some time ago.'

'How long ago?' I asked.

He thought for a moment. 'Oh, I've been in the shop for over a year now. Haven't knocked on a door for over a year. I miss it, too, you know—miss it very much. Used to do very, very well on the road . . .'

He yacked away about his accomplishments until I thought my ears would burst and I was just going to kill him when we arrived at the house.

'Right, now,' he said, 'got your dem cloths and your H.P. forms? Checked your machines, have you? Always check your machines before going into the house . . .'

He was getting truly on my wick, I can tell you.

He charged up to the front door and snapped at the knocker and was grinning all over his face with what he probably thought was charm. Actually he looked critically ill.

The door opened and a nice little body stood there wondering who was trying to bash her front door down.

'Good morning, madam!' gushed O'Neill. 'We are from . . .' So help me, he was doing all the chat!

Well, we got inside the house and he started spraying his personality around like Flit, trying to impress somebody or other, and the little old lady was looking at him as if she was trying to remember something.

'Right, Mr Tobin, put your machine over here, there's a good chap. Now, madam, did you say you had a machine already?'

'Er . . . yes . . .' she said. 'I've got an old Singer treadle.'

Her face was all screwed up with some very heavy thinking.

'Good ... splendid ...' said O'Neill. 'That's right, Mr Tobin, plug it in there and put the case cover on the floor ...'

He was doing his nut—going at it hammer and tongs.

'Now, madam, if you'd care to sit down here ...'

''Ere!' she said suddenly, peering at O'Neill closely. 'I know you now. I thought I recognized you the moment you came in. You're Mr O'Neill, aren't you?'

'Er ... yes, madam.'

He looked dead worried.

'Ah, yes, I remember now,' she said accusingly. 'You came 'ere two years ago trying to sell me a big expensive machine! You sold me this 'ere little one and then you tried to pull a fast one ...'

She chucked us out.

I never said a word going back in the car. O'Neill laughed it off, of course, and tried to turn the whole thing into a big joke.

'Ha, well would you believe it, Russ ...' (!) '... fancy a thing like that happening. Mind you, it wouldn't happen again in a thousand years ...'

I didn't say a word. I just let him stew in his own big-headed cock-up and listened to him trying to convince himself.

When I let him out of the car back at the shop he said, 'Well, go to it, Russ. See if you can't pull back next week.'

And, by golly, I did too—with a vengeance. I think the incident must have restored my sense of humour or something because I did eleven machines that week—and I met Milly!

It happened at one of our away cricket matches. We were playing a team over in the Wirral that Saturday and I drove over there, feeling terribly superior to the poor sods who had had to go by train.

Well, it was a pretty good match for the first half. We were fielding and suddenly I got lucky with the ball and bowled out half of their fellows for next to nothing. Anyway, while I was fielding and not bowling I was having a casual look around the spectators who were sitting in deck chairs outside the pavilion and suddenly I spotted this gorgeous apparition in a blue cotton dress.

She had legs up to her armpits and the way she was sitting in the deck chair I could see most of them. And surprise, surprise, when my eyes got up to her face that was just peachy too.

131

I got so fascinated by this little angel that I was standing there gawking and the ball trickled right past me and went for a boundary, which prompted some wiseacre to yell out, 'Wake up, dozey!' and about four hundred people fell about laughing.

During the interval we all crowded round the refreshment table in the pavilion and I had one eye on my lettuce sandwich, which was balancing on my cup of tea together with a rock cake and a chocolate biscuit, and the other eye doing a radar scan for Miss Legs. And then I spotted her—and she was actually talking to one of our fellows—Rodney Hamilton. Of all people, Rodney Hamilton, who could never be regarded as the lover type by any stretch of the imagination. He was short, dumpy, had buck-teeth and he couldn't even bat.

So I sort of sidled over and flipped a quick, 'Hi, Rodney! Well played!' which was an outrageous liberty really because he'd dropped three catches in the first half and I'd forgotten all about them until I'd said it. He didn't seem to notice, though, because he had eyes, ears and heart only for Miss Legs.

'Hi, Russ,' he said, not really caring.

I caught Miss Legs' eye and said a very proper, 'How d'you do?' and she smiled and dropped her eyes as women do when they really want to look at you.

Rodney obviously wasn't going to introduce me, so I said to her, en passant, as it were, 'Enjoying the game?'

The eyes came up all smiling. 'Yes, thank you.'

Nice! Nicely spoken and very friendly and the eyes were now darting all over me, taking in teeth, hair, physique . . .

Rodney knew he was licked.

'Er . . . this is Russ Tobin,' he said to her, quite formally. He turned to me. 'This is a friend of mine, Miss Millicent Warwick.'

She laughed at him. 'Oh, don't be so formal, Rodney.' She hung out a pretty little hand to me. 'Just plain Millie will do.'

I took the hand and gave it a little squeeze.

'Millie, perhaps,' I said, 'but certainly not plain.'

She laughed and I pulled a conspiratorial face at Rodney as though we were all lads together. He wasn't fooled for a second. He gave me a smeer, which is half-way between a smile and a sneer, and took Millie's arm.

'Shall we go to the table, Millie?' he said pointedly.

'Er . . . yes,' she said, very unconvincingly and flashed me a smile of regret.

But yours truly was never defeated that easily—especially by a berk like Rodney Hamilton. During the second half when we were batting I kept close tabs on them and when Rodney went in to bat I was in there like a shot.

She was sitting in the deck chair again and Rodney had hardly taken middle and leg before I said, 'Oh, hello there!' as if I'd just stumbled into her. 'Mind if I sit down?'

She gave me a big smile. 'No, please do.'

I squatted on the grass by her side.

'You bowled very well,' she said.

'Oh, d'you think so? Thank you.'

'How many wickets did you get?'

I pretended to think. 'Er ... oh, five or six, I think,' I said off-handedly, knowing damn well it was five for an average of 7·534 runs recurring. 'Do you ... er ... come to many games, Millie?'

'No, this is my first really.'

'Oh?'

She laughed. 'I've only taken it up since I met Rodney.'

I laughed too. 'Hm, when was that exactly?'

'Last Thursday.'

'What—d'you mean the Thursday just gone?'

'Yes.'

'Oh, I see ... I took it you'd known each other a long time.'

'No—only three days.'

There was a little silence during which Rodney flashed at the ball outside his off stump, missed, and nearly decapitated the wicketkeeper.

'You play every week, I suppose,' she said.

'Well, when I have time,' I said with just the right touch of martyrdom in the voice. 'Business, you know ...'

'Oh, what business is that?'

'Sewing machines. I sell them.'

She shot round in the deck chair and I got a glorious eyeful of thigh that stretched away from her kneecap like the M.1.

'Really! How marvellous!'

Here we go again.

'Why, are you interested ...?'

'Oh, yes! I've been thinking about getting one for ages. I've been looking at the Elna and the Necchi and the Singer but I can't make up my mind which one to buy. What do you sell?'

133

'The best—the Ritebuy Major.'

She looked blank. 'I don't think I've heard of that one.'

I shook my head. 'No, it's not advertised like the others. That's why we can sell it so cheaply.'

'How much is it?'

I thought for a moment. 'Look, how about me coming round and giving you a demonstration. Any time, day or night and absolutely no obligation.'

'Oh, yes,' she said. 'That'd be super!'

'Right . . . hang on. I'll get a pencil and take your address.'

Well, I got all the pertinent facts from her (she had a room in a boarding house and the landlady was most understanding —whatever that meant) and I promised to pop round on Monday evening about seven.

Just then Rodney was out so I went in to bat and as the bowler was running up for the very first ball Millie happened to cross her legs and I was bowled neck and crop.

On the Monday I'd had a pretty fair day with two machines in the bag so by the time I drove up to Millie's place I was feeling on top of the world.

I rang the bell and a funny old Jewish lady came to the door and said, 'Hello! Will you come in, please? You're expected already.' Nice soul.

I stepped into the hallway and Millie was at the top of the stairs waiting for me.

'Thank you, Mrs Leyevski,' she called down. 'Come on up, Russ.'

I thumped up the stairs with the Major, and Millie showed me into a smallish but pretty room which was almost entirely filled by the most comfortable-looking double bed I've ever . . . well, seen. There was an armchair and a chest of drawers and that was about it.

'No table?' I asked her.

'Here—in the kitchen,' she said.

We went through the bedroom and into a fairly big old-fashioned kitchen which must have been converted from a bed-room at some time or other.

'How about some coffee?' she said.

Nice, isn't it, how they always want to feed you?

'Yes, thank you.'

While she was making the coffee I was getting the Major all set up and then I ran through a dem for her. She was very impressed.

'It's lovely, Russ,' she said excitedly. 'Now show me how it zig-zags!'

Suddenly I could smell disaster again.

'Eh?'

'Show me how it zig-zags.'

'I'm . . . afraid it doesn't.'

Her face dropped. 'Oh, Russ . . . I'm so sorry, I should have told you. I need one that does all sorts of fancy stitching. It's for the costumes, you see . . .'

'What sort of costumes?'

She laughed. 'Well, I teach ballet and the children . . .'

'Do you?' I said.

Now, that explained the legs!

'. . . I wanted to make the children's costumes . . . oh, I'm so sorry—you came all this way for nothing . . .'

I grinned at her and patted her hand to make her feel better.

'I wouldn't say that,' I said. 'You can dance for me.'

She threw back her head and laughed. 'In this place? You're joking!'

'No, I'm not. We can move the table to one side . . .'

'And ballet dance!' she laughed. 'I'd knock all the cups off the shelf.'

'Well, just show me the movements, then. I'm very interested.'

Ooh, what a whopper!

'Really?'

'Yes.'

She thought about it for a second and then shook her head.

'Well, I certainly can't show you in this!' she said, holding her dress out. 'I have to dance in tights.'

'So—put them on.'

She shook her head and laughed. 'No, I couldn't . . .'

What she was actually saying was 'talk me into it.' So I did.

'Oh, all right, then. But if Mrs Leyevski comes up she'll have a fit.'

'I thought you said she was very understanding?'

She gave me the eyes and said, 'Nobody is *that* understanding.'

She got up from the table and made for the bedroom.

'And you stay in here. No peeping!'

I crossed my heart.

She went into the bedroom and I heard a lot of rustling of clothes and then in a few minutes the door flung open and there she was, standing poised on her tip-toes, her wonderful legs encased in black tights and her hands held gracefully over her head. On the top she had a thin cotton shirt-blouse which in this position was failing delightfully to contain her goodly sized bust.

'Tra-la!' she sang.

I applauded.

She came down out of the pose. 'Now you can get the record player from the bedroom—it's under the bed—and put it on this table. I must have music.'

I did just that and then she selected some ballet music from a stack of discs which she kept in the kitchen cupboard and put it on.

'First, I'll show you the positions,' she said seriously.

'How many are there?'

'Six.'

'Is that all? I always heard there were forty-two,' I said, pulling her leg. 'No, forty-three—if you include the "washing basket from the chandelier way".'

She gave me a very knowing look and said, 'Down boy! I was referring to ballet positions.'

So away she went and of course I didn't know what she was talking about most of the time, I was just watching the movement of her strong, perfect body and those incredibly long legs.

She really was something to watch. She moved in a graceful, sensuous way, just like a cat—controlled and lithe without seeming muscular, and she got into positions I didn't think were humanly possible. I was having the time of my life.

At the end of the demonstration she curtsied gracefully and I clapped and gave her a rose from the flower vase.

'What other records have you got?' I asked.

She pointed to the stack on the cupboard. 'Help yourself, I'm going to change.'

'No . . . don't!'

She stopped half-way to the door and turned round slowly, giving me a mock suspicious glower.

'Oh, and why not?'

'Because I want you to show me just one more step.'

'What's that?'

'Just a sec.'

I riffed through the pile of L.P.s and found a Tony Bennett that was just right for the occasion—slow, dreamy and soulful.

'What are you putting on?' she asked from the doorway.

'Chopin's Prelude in the right key but the wrong flat,' I said, slipping the stylus across.

'Ai dern't recall 'avin' that one,' she joked.

Up came Mr Bennett all cool and warm at the same time and she tutted at me and came across into my outstretched arms.

Just for a minute she was a little bit reserved and held her tights away from me, but during the second number her tum came against mine, liked it and stayed—and by the third track she was eating me alive.

We must have danced through two whole L.P.s before we made the slow, crawly exodus from the kitchen and into the bedroom. Then I lifted her up and laid her gently on the bed.

'No, we shouldn't . . .' she murmured. 'Mrs Leyevski . . .'

I looked astounded. 'Oh, I'm not coming in. I'm going home.'

'You do and I'll scream,' she said viciously.

I grinned at her. 'What time does Mrs Leyevski go to bed?'

'About nine.'

I looked at my watch. 'Then she's there now.'

She seemed to relax but then immediately she became tense again. 'No, I'll have to see you out. She'll be wondering . . .'

'And then I creep back again?'

She nodded slowly but her breath was coming quickly with excitement.

'O.K.,' I said. 'I'll even drive the car down the street and then walk back.'

We made a fair bit of noise saying goodnight going down the stairs and Millie pointed that the light under the front downstairs room meant that Mrs Leyevski was still awake.

She opened the door to the street and said quite loudly, 'Goodnight, Russ. Thank you so much for coming round.'

She watched me off the premises and I started the car and drove down the street for maybe fifty yards and then parked it. I locked it and ran full pelt back again on tiptoe, half expecting that Millie would have disappeared and the door would be closed. But there she was, peeping through the gap in the door and 'shush-ing' me with her finger to her lips.

As I approached the door she pointed down at my shoes, so

137

I took them off and slipped silently into the hall.

For a moment we stood there in the dark, listening to Mrs Leyevski having a good cough and to my own heart banging away like a thrashing machine. Then Millie started up the stairs, stepped lightly on her tiptoes, and I followed.

There were more steps than in the Eiffel Tower and every one of the perishers squeaked. But, at last, a final step into Millie's room and we threw our arms around each other and roared with silent laughter.

'Doesn't she ever come up here at night?' I whispered.

Millie shook her head and snuggled up against me and we danced like that for a bit, without music, just to get back into the mood again. Well, you just can't leap into bed after all that excitement, can you? You've got to let things slip back slowly into a nice, lazy romantic mood, otherwise the whole thing is laughable and soulless.

In about three minutes they'd slipped right back.

We left a tiny bedside light on but put it down on the floor so that it cast a nice warm glow against the ceiling and then reflected back on to the bed. So much nicer than direct lighting. I'm a stickler for the right sort of lighting, you know. It makes all the difference in the world. I mean how can you start being artistic if there's a dirty great 150-watt bulb hitting you in the eye and exposing all the tiny, human imperfections in the girl's skin? I was once put right off a very beautiful little custard at a very crucial moment just because the bedside light exposed a big blackhead on the end of her nose, and I always swore after that that I'd get the lighting right before I organized anything else.

'How the devil d'you get these tights off?' I said, and she giggled.

'You shouldn't have asked me to put them on.'

'That's history—now is now!'

'I'm not going to help you. You'll just have to struggle.'

I could tell right then that she liked a bit of a wrestle. Some do, some don't. This one was a bit butch.

We had a whale of a time. You've no idea what positions we got into before those tights were keeping my trousers company on the floor. But she'd stated her case—laid down the pattern of desire, so to speak, and, being a gentleman, I obliged. She liked to play—nothing too direct—here, there and everywhere. Parry, thrust, feint, plunge, withdraw, attack, have a breather.

I was coming in on one particularly sneaky line of attack

138

when her eyes suddenly went wide open and she shush-ed me. We both hung suspended and listened.

The stairs were creaking!

'Oh, Lord!' she whispered.

We searched the room in panic but we already knew there wasn't a place to hide. Then she had it.

'Down there!' she breathed, pointing at the gap between the bed and the wall. It was about a foot wide.

'Eh!'

'Go on!'

I took a deep breath and fell over the side, squeezing down until I was flattened between the bed and the wall. When I was touching the floor with my shoulder she threw some bedclothes into the gap and then I heard her get off the bed and slip her dressing gown on and start singing to herself as she tidied our clothes off the floor. Great presence of mind, this kid.

There was a creak outside the door.

'Millie, darlin' . . . are you asleep?'

Bright and breezy, Millie answered. 'No, Mrs Leyevski, did you want me?'

'Just for a moment, darlin', yes.'

My nose was flattened against the mattress and I was gasping for breath through my mouth.

'Sssshh!' hissed Millie.

I heard the door open.

'Your young man gone, has he?' I could see the old girl's beady eyes flashing round the bedroom and the kitchen.

'Oh, yes, ages ago,' laughed Millie.

The old girl laughed too. 'Now, isn't that funny? I could have sworn I heard you two laughing together just now . . .'

Millie laughed again. 'Oh, no—it must have been my radio. Mrs Leyevski. I had my radio on.'

'Ah, that was it . . . no, all I wanted to ask you was whether you liked the machine or not.'

I felt an ominous tickle on my right foot and I broke out in an ice-cold sweat. If there's one thing I hate and detest above all others it's bleeding spiders. Great filthy things—even the tiny ones. If that was a spider on my foot I'd just have to give myself up . . .

'No, I'm afraid it wouldn't do, Mrs Leyevski. It wouldn't zig-zag.'

'Wouldn't zig-zag?' said the old girl in her sing-song. 'Oh, well, that's no good, is it, darlin'. A machine's no good these days unless it zig-zags . . .'

Oh, go to bed, you silly old boot.

That tickle was getting higher! It was a spider, I just knew it. About nine inches across and hairy as a brush . . .

'Oh, well, I'll say goodnight, Millie. You were in bed, already?'

She must have been looking straight at me though she didn't know it. Or did she? These old birds are very cunning, you know.

'Yes!' said Millie, a little too readily, I thought. 'I was . . . I felt a bit tired so I thought I'd have an early night.'

'Ah, what it is to be able to sleep,' sighed the old cod. 'I can't sleep any more . . .' She started backing away towards the stairs. '. . . I shall probably be reading the papers until four o'clock in the morning . . .' She started down the stairs. '. . . Well, goodnight, darlin' . . .'

That damned spider was nibbling my things!

'Goodnight, Mrs Leyevski.'

'Get a good night's sleep, now . . .'

'Yes, I will.'

Oh, close the friggin' door, Millie, and let me get rid of this great, fat, hairy spider . . .

She did finally close it and I whispered, 'Pull the bed out, for God's sake, I can't get up!'

She heaved the bed away from the wall and I fell on to my knees—starkers, too. I ask you! And then I saw it! The obscene, fluttering, pulsating mass of diabolical fiendishness that had nearly stopped my heart down there in Death Valley —it was a minute white moth about a billionth of an inch long. I felt a right twit.

I stood up and Millie went into hysterics, holding her hand over her mouth while the tears rolled down her cheeks. I was covered in fluff and there was one particularly large piece . . . Well, I didn't think it was all that funny.

I removed the fluff and eventually got back into bed but I could tell Millie had gone off, so to speak. She was giggling hysterically and I suspected deep shock. So we put on some clothes and Millie made some coffee and we sat in the kitchen and drank it.

'How am I going to get out?' I whispered. 'The old girl says she doesn't sleep.'

She shrugged and grinned at me—still in shock, see.

'You'll have to stay all night,' she said.

'Eh!'

'Do you mind?' she said, all sexy, and I could tell she was coming round.

'No, don't be daft, but how do I get out tomorrow morning?'

Mrs Leyevski goes out shopping at nine. You just walk out when she's gone.'

'Is there nobody else in the house?'

She nodded. 'Her son—but he goes out at eight.'

'What time do you leave?'

'I go at eight, too.'

'You mean I'll be here for an hour by myself?'

She laughed. 'You'll be all right. Mrs Leyevski never comes up here. I do my own room.'

I smiled sarcastically. 'I seem to recall you saying that earlier on—and up she popped.'

She grinned. 'Special occasion. Want to go to bed?'

Just like that.

Oh, it was a lovely night—adventurous, if you know what I mean. Hither and thither, tooth and nail; tote that barge and lift that bale. I learned a great deal from Millie. It really is quite extraordinary the positions the human body can assume when the mind is applied properly. Mind you, I would add a smidgin of caution because at one point I got the most diabolical cramp and nearly did myself a terrible injury. So do take care.

Came the morn and I woke up with the sun streaming through the window on to my face. It was all quite beautiful—until I remembered where I was. I sat up in bed and looked down at Millie; she was lying with her back to me, all relaxed and warm and soft like a great cuddly kitten. Aren't women wonderful—I mean, really? Can you imagine anything more delectable than a young, healthy, good-looking, well-built woman who has all her marbles and isn't averse to letting you play with them? that's providing you're a fella, of course!

Millie looked a treat—so much so that I couldn't resist her and I cuddled into her and she moaned nicely and tried to back me on to the landing.

'Goood mooorning,' she murmured, all sleepy and gorgeous 'What time is it?'

'Nearly seven,' I said.

'Ooooh,' she moaned lazily. 'I'll have to get up.' She yawned and got me at it, too.

'Ten minutes?' I said in her ear.

'Mmmmm!' she went, all wriggly and got me off the starting blocks again.

There is nothing nicer than breakfast in bed. No—not the full
British bit from grapefruit to marmalade, but a delicate,
leisurely Continental snippet. Nothing too strenuous that
leaves you crippled for the day, but a light titillating of the
senses that sets you up spiritually to face the rigours . . . oh, I
don't know what the hell I'm talking about, but whatever
Millie and I had in the next ten minutes was just dandy.

I lay in bed and watched her get dressed after she'd had a
quick bath. It was like watching a strip-tease in reverse and
just as enjoyable. This girl really knew how to move.

'What would you like for breakfast,' she said, fastening her
suspender.

'You again.'

She pretended to be serious—now that she'd got all her
clothes on.

'Seriously,' she said.

'Oh, nothing too much,' I said languidly. 'Perhaps just a
pate de fois gras butty and a cup of tea.'

She took a swipe at me and went into the kitchen. 'You'll
get toast and marmalade and like it. Go and have a bath.'

After breakfast she said, 'About nine o'clock, go out on to
the landing and listen for Mrs Leyevski going out and then
give her five minutes—just in case she stops to talk with the
woman next door.'

'Roger!' I said.

'And do be careful when you leave. Have a peep up and
down the street in case she's forgotten something and is on her
way back.'

'Yes, ma'am.'

'And another thing . . .'

'Yes, ma'am?'

She grinned at me and put her hand out to be held. 'I think
you're lovely.'

I laughed at her and kissed her fingers.

'I think I'm lovely, too,' I joked. 'It was fun, eh?'

She growled like a dog. I looked at my watch and nodded
towards the bedroom. 'Let's go back, you've got five minutes.'

She laughed and said, 'Just for that you can wash up.'

I saw her out of the door and she popped her head back and
gave me a nice little kiss that was full of meaning.

' 'Bye,' she whispered. 'See you.'

'You bet your tights,' I said.

And then she was gone. The place seemed funny after that. They do, don't they, other people's rooms and houses when the owners aren't there? They're full of little bits and pieces that obviously mean so much to them but not a blind thing to you and you feel out of it somehow. And the silence is shattering.

I sat on the bed and looked at my watch eight thousand times in the first fifteen minutes. I tried to read a magazine but that didn't work and then, as I was just flicking over the pages, I vaguely heard the front door bell go. Then I heard Mrs Leveyski open the door and a man's voice started rumbling. And then the stairs started squeaking again!

Well, there was only one thing for it. Back to the fluff!

I quickly pulled the bed out from the wall and once again squeezed down into the gap and pulled the drooping counterpane over me. Ah, how nice it was to be back again. Seemed ages since I was last there.

The door opened.

'And this is my lodger's room,' said Mrs Leyevski. 'It hasn't been done for nearly three years so I think we'd better have this done, too.'

'Yes, thank you, madam,' said the bloke. 'Wallpaper? ... emulsion paint?'

'Oh, I think wallpaper ... but I also think I'll let Miss Warwick choose it herself. She's such a nice young lady and I think she'd appreciate choosing her own paper.'

'Rightee ho, madam. I'll bring the sample books round for the young lady this evening. Now, I'll just measure up...'

I heard him flicking a steel tape measure around the walls and whistling in a breathy, tuneless way as he went. Then he said, 'No plaster defects, are there, madam?—behind the bed, maybe?'

My moment had come, I just knew it. Oh, the horror of it. He'd yank the bed away and there I'd be—standing there as helpless as a spare bloke at a sex orgy. I'd have to run for the stairs with them running after me shouting, 'Stop thief!' or something equally ridiculous. Or maybe I'd just grin at Mrs Leyevski and say, 'Just popped back for my reel of white cotton. Rolled under the bed, you know.'

How did I get myself into these messes? Nothing was simple and straightforward these days—always terrible complications. Well, I knew one thing for certain—if I got out of this one alive, I would never, never get into another! But, please, for Millie's sake—and mine—please make them go away!

'No, nothing like that, Mr Rankin,' said dear, sweet, kind, intelligent Mrs Leyevski. 'But do have a look if you want to. I'll give you a hand with the bed . . .'

'No, it's quite all right, madam. I'll take your word for it. Right, well that's all for now. I'll get your estimate worked out and I'll drop the samples round this evening . . .'

I heard them stomping down the stairs and at that moment there was no sweeter sound in the world. I stayed put until the front door closed behind Rankin and then I crept out.

My midnight blue suit was more of a lunch-time grey. I was covered in fluff. I found a clothes-brush in the kitchen and scrubbed most of it off but it still looked pretty manky. Then at nine o'clock I crept out on to the landing.

Right on the button Mrs Leyevski came out of her room and opened the front door. Then she paused, turned away from the door and stood at the bottom of the stairs.

'Oh, Mr Tobin!' she shouted. 'I'm going shopping so you can come down now. Make sure you close the door properly, won't you?'

THIRTEEN

Well, I'd learned my lesson, I can tell you. No more complications for me! From now on it was going to be strictly business all the way. No romances, no side-orders of monkey business, no dilettanting when I should have been demming—nothing! Just business.

Oh, I didn't desert the darlings, don't think that. I'm not that sort of bloke. No, I took Gloria to the pictures; I went across to New Brighton on the ferry with Samantha and had a giggle in the fairground; I called in on Helen and Chris and took them some flowers; and I went to the Empire with Millie to see a musical.

Mind you, I'm not saying that these little visitations were purely platonic—that'd be rubbish, wouldn't it?—but I am saying that they were strictly extra-curricula, after-hours sorties that had nothing to do with the business of selling sewing machines. In that respect I had turned over a new leaf completely and, by gum, wasn't that side of life going well! In the third week of September I was actually top salesman with thirteen machines (and not one feminine conquest that I can recall) to my credit and I was able to pay off the final instalment on the car. Life indeed looked rosy and just when I was beginning to think that nothing could come along to make it otherwise I had to go and meet Peter and Francis. It was a very nasty experience, I can tell you.

It was a sweet little house in a quiet mews and it stood out from the others like a poppy in a cornfield. The white pebble-dash had been Snowcemed very recently and the plain glass in the bay windows had been replaced with leaded lights which gave it a cottagey appearance.

Under the windows were yellow boxes of bright pink petunias and yellow antirrhinums which really brought the house to life and on the wall by the glass front door was a brass coach-lamp which gleamed in the late afternoon sun.

A dolly little love nest for some lucky couple.

As I stood on the doorstep in the warm sun I marvelled at the quiet and the tranquillity of the cul-de-sac—so near to the madding city and yet so far away. All was peace.

The door opened and a very pretty young man stood there, looking me over with disturbing approbation shining in his big blue eyes.

'Hellooo!' he drawled, with a damn-sight more meaning than Samantha got out of it.

Well, there's only one way to deal with this situation and that's to go real butch—talk tough from the side of your mouth like Bogart and let them know right from the start that you're a member of a very different club. If you smile just once it takes you an hour to regain lost ground.

'How d'you do? Mr Thomas?' I said gruffly. Oh, I can be gruff, I'll tell you. Especially with so much at stake.

In answer he stepped to one side like a ballet dancer and gestured me in with a long, languid arm.

He was dressed to kill—and by the way he was looking at me I had a pretty good idea who he had in mind for his next victim. From his fair curly hair to his French canvas casuals he was Carnaby Street gone berserk. Two-tone blue polo-neck sweater in the finest wool; grey fleck hipsters as slim as a pipe and so tight you could see all of his hors-d'œuvre and three-quarters of the meat course; and a couple of gold rings on his delicate fingers that must have made it difficult for him to lift his arm up. He was a dilly.

'What, pray, is your name?' he said, giving me the teeth and the eyelashes.

'Tobin,' I growled.

'What . . . a delightful name. Tobin what?'

'Tobin nothing. It's Russell Tobin.'

He looked sad. 'Oh, what a shame. Do go into the lounge, Mr Tobin.'

'After you, Mr Thomas.'

It's always best to keep these boys in front of you.

With a gesture of sheer delight he ponced off down the very arty hallway, swinging his hands wide of his sides and keeping his elbows tucked into his waist.

I had a quick look around the hall. It was spotlessly clean and very colourful—filled with prints of modern paintings and more plant life than the Burma jungle. It smelt like a woman's handbag.

The lounge was as big as the house would let it be which wasn't very, and it ran right through from the front to the back. It was carpeted wall-to-wall with thick, white, curly

146

money and the deep-blue three-piece suite was just as expensive. There were more gay prints on the walls.

Sitting at a small dining table at the far end of the room and gazing in rapture at some sketches on men's clothing was a dark-haired fellow about Thomas's age. He was dark-skinned, too, and could either have been Spanish or just back from his holidays in Blackpool. At first glance he seemed pretty normal and much less effeminate than his boy-friend but he went and spoilt it by saying 'Hellooo' just like Thomas.

He rose from his chair (meaning he just didn't get up) and floated across to us, pulling down his two-tone grey sweater around his bum as he came. He had on the same sort of hipsters as Thomas, but in blue, so that if they'd been lying head-and-tail the two fellows would have matched——which, come to think of it, was probably what they had in mind.

'This is Mr Tobin, Francis,' said Thomas. And then he said irritably, 'Oh, all this formality. My name is Peter, his is Francis and you're Russell. Now, come and put your sewing machine over on the table, Russell, it must be frightfully heavy for you holding it like that.'

He swished away and cleared the pile of designs into a tidy heap and then gestured delicately to the table.

'Pop it down there, ducky, and we'll have a look at it. D'you want a plug?'

I wasn't too sure about that one but there appeared to be no ulterior motive behind the question so I said 'Yes.'

Hitching up his hipsters he dropped to the floor with the cord and popped under the table and waved his bottom at the ceiling while he was plugging it in. I heard a sharp intake of breath in my right ear and turned round quickly to find Francis watching Peter's contortions with an expression of tender lust.

He saw my look, dragged his eyes away and gave a bashful giggle and blushed.

'There we are,' said Peter, backing out from under. 'Now, Francis, get some chairs.'

They bustled around making me comfortable and then I took the cover off the Minor.

'Oh, I say, it's terribly small, isn't it, Russell,' said Peter.

'Frightfully dinky,' said Francis.

I shrugged. 'Depends what you want it for.'

Peter smiled at his soul mate and reached for the pile of designs.

'Take a look at these,' he said proudly. 'These are Francis's

147

own designs. Don't you think they're gorgeous?'

I flipped through the illustrations and saw a dozen variations of outrageously mod suits and shirts which had more frills and fol-de-rols than a Victorian sideboard.

'What . . . do you think of those?' said Peter breathlessly.

'Dinky,' I said and Francis giggled.

'You see,' explained Peter, 'we run a gent's boutique in town but so far we've only sold other people's gear. So we thought it was about time we started designing our own and we want a machine to make them up—ever so roughly, mind you—and then, if they're successful, we'll get them made professionally. See what I mean?'

'What an excellent idea,' I said.

'Yes, we thought so,' said Francis, still looking doubtfully at the Minor. 'But somehow, ducky . . .'

'You think this is too small,' I finished for him.

'Oh, yes, I do think so. Haven't you anything larger?'

'Yes, I have,' I said. 'And more expensive.'

'Oh . . . naturally,' said Francis. 'Do bring it in and let us have a peep!'

I was beginning to like these two—despite their religion. There was something buoyant and lighthearted about them that lifted you up and made you want to laugh with them.

'I'll go and get it,' I said.

Francis leapt from his chair and drew mine away from me with an exaggerated gesture of olde worlde charm. So I bowed my appreciation to him and we all had a good laugh.

'Don't be long!' he chuckled.

Back at the car I had a good laugh to myself about these two. I'd never before met such a pair of outrageous queens and I must admit that in the past I'd always taken a very intolerant line about such gentlemen, always been very ready to condemn. And yet here I was quite enjoying their company and having a lot of fun.

I lugged the Major back into the house and the two of them fussed around helping me, shoving the Minor to one side and plugging in the Major (this time both of them went under the table and had a lovely time trying to plug it in).

'There,' said Peter, 'it's all yours, love.'

They got up and sorted themselves out like a couple of women putting their corsets straight.

I took off the cover.

'Ooooh . . . I say! . . .' said Francis.

'Fran . . . cis!' said Peter. 'Oh, now that's so much better.'

'It's expensive,' I warned them.

Francis ran his fingers delicately over the machine as though it was a Wedgwood vase. 'How much precisely?'

'Forty-nine pounds ten,' I said.

I expected a bit of reaction but there wasn't any; they just kept looking at the machine and I wondered if they were in deep shock.

'Of course ...' I went on quickly, '... we do offer easy payments...'

Peter tossed his head. 'Oh, no, ducky, we never touch never-never. Cash on the line is our motto—pay as we go, isn't that right, Francis?'

'Quite right, angel,' said Francis. 'Pay as we go.' He turned to me. 'What does it do, Russell? Could we have a little dem, do you think? Would you mind?'

I laughed. 'You can have a big one if you want it.'

I started getting the dem cloth out and generally getting settled down and Peter said, 'Oooh, Francis, shall we ask Russell what he thinks of you know what?' He cocked his head towards the kitchen door.

'Mm? ... oh, yes, yes, by all means,' he laughed. 'Bring in three, lovey.'

I looked at them, puzzled, but they weren't going to tell me any more for the time being.

Peter went into the kitchen and I could hear a chinking of glasses and a slurping of liquid being poured and so on, and then he came back with three punch-cups on a little tray.

'Russell,' he said excitedly, 'we'd like you to give us your candid opinion about this. It's Francis's own creation and we think it's divine. Do tell us what you think of it.'

He offered me a cup and gave one to Francis and took one himself. Then he raised his and said, 'To our successful new venture!'

Now I'm not a great one for punch. It always seems to me to be a shocking waste of several good liquors to mix them all up together with the seemingly express purpose of killing all their individual tastes and producing a sneakily intoxicating mess that tastes of apple juice. I'd much rather drink them all separately and then have an apple juice chaser. However, I could sense a sale being very imminent and I didn't want to hurt their sensitive souls, so I took a decent-sized gulp to get it over with quickly.

It tasted, of course, like apple juice with just the tiniest tingle on the tonsils as it slipped over the edge.

'Delicious!' I said.

They were ecstatic. 'Really! You really think so, Russell?'

'Hmm!' I mumbled and finished the cup.

'Oooops! Steady!' laughed Peter. 'It's quite potent, you know.'

'I wouldn't have guessed it,' I said. 'Smoothness itself.'

'Another?' said Peter, teasingly.

I shrugged. 'Mm, O.K.'

They finished theirs, too, and Peter almost ran into the kitchen with empty glasses.

'We're having a little "soiree" this evening,' said Francis. 'Just a few close friends. It's our anniversary, you see.'

He didn't say what of and I didn't pursue the matter.

'. . . so I thought up this little drink for us all and I think it ought to go down rather well, don't you?'

'Very,' I said.

Peter came back, walking very carefully so the drinks wouldn't spill.

'Here we are. So glad you like it, Russell.'

'I was just telling him about our little get-together tonight,' said Francis.

Peter took a sip and tried to talk at the same time. 'Mm . . . yes . . . would you like to come, Russell? You'll be more than welcome, I'm sure. Some very interesting people coming— artists . . . designers . . . even an actor or two.'

'Well, that's very kind . . .'

'Oh, do stay,' pleaded Francis. 'You've been so very nice. I'm sure you'd fit in.'

I took another gulp of the apple-jack. Strange! I could have sworn the Major rose an inch off the table on its own accord. I blinked several times and tried to get rid of the mellow haze that was slowly falling down the inside of my head.

'Phew!' I said. 'What did you put in that punch?'

Peter giggled. 'Ah ha! Told you, didn't I. You must always treat Francis's little concoctions with the greatest respect.'

'What's in it?' I said.

Francis shrugged. 'Oh, just a little brandy . . .'

'And?'

'. . . a little Vodka . . .'

'And . . .'

'. . . a smidgin of rough cider . . .'

150

'And?'

Francis laughed. 'Oh, I can't remember all of it. Just bits and pieces.'

'You really should have written it down,' scolded Peter. 'This is certainly your best yet.'

'What's the base?' I asked. 'Lighter fluid?'

They both hooted with laughter.

'Well,' I said, 'I'd better show you how this machine works while I can still see it. Firstly, the floating foot. Now, this enables you to . . .'

And I was off on the dem.

In the next half hour I'd finished that drink and had another two and I seemed to be floating about three inches off the chair. The room and the machine and the two lads were all nebulous things, drifting about on invisible supports like goldfish in a bowl. When they spoke their voices seemed to reach me down a long, echoing tunnel and when I replied the voice came from someone else standing about a foot to my left and slightly behind. All of which is a bloody long-winded way of saying I was stoned.

I don't know what time the guests started arriving, but I do know that suddenly I found myself talking to a weird, dedicated face with glasses and a beard and I remember being astounded that Peter—or Francis—could have changed so drastically in the last hour or so.

'Do you dabble?' the face said earnestly and emptied a glass of punch into itself.

'I beg your pardon?'

'Paint? Do you paint, man?' it said.

'Oh . . . oh, yes.'

'What?'

'Bathrooms.'

'Kinky!'

The left eye gave me a wink and disappeared towards the kitchen.

'This is Russell,' Francis was saying behind me and I turned to shake the podgy hand of a revolting-looking individual with white curly hair and a bamboo cigarette-holder.

'Charmed, I'm sure . . .' it said and wiggled its lips at me.

'Yes,' I said and dropped the hand smartly.

'Ronnie's in underwear,' explained Francis.

'Aren't we all,' I said, and they giggled like a couple of schoolgirls in the boys' changing room.

'Not for long, ducky,' said Ronnie, and if I hadn't been so stoned I'd have taken more notice and cleared out right there and then.

Francis and Ronnie wandered out of my sight and I continued to turn round and round on the spot hoping to find something stationary and familiar to focus on—something like a wall, perhaps.

The kitchen door eventually came to my rescue so I tottered off towards it feeling like Ping, the Elastic Man, and somehow reached the bunch bowl.

'What can I do for you, lover?' said a tall, skinny bloke in a puce sweater and maroon slacks. He had the punch ladle in his hand and looked like one of the Macbeth witches stooping over her cauldron.

I stuck my empty cup at him, meaning him to take it from me, but he misunderstood and slopped in another bucketful.

'Have you seen it before?' he murmured, resting his hand on my free arm.

I looked at him intently, trying to get his face into focus. 'The punch?' I said.

He tutted and flung his eyelashes at the ceiling. 'No, silly, the film?' His voice was low and excited. I shook his hand off and stepped back a foot or two.

'What film?'

'Oh, for heaven's sake . . .' he said, disgusted. 'Don't you know about it?'

I shook my head and thought it was going to drop off into the punch.

'Francis has got hold of the new one!' he whispered. '. . . you know—"Lash McTaggart Meets The Chief Whip"! Ve . . . ry good, from what I've heard. Everyone's talking about it.'

'Really?'

'Even better than his last one "On The Stroke of Nine"—did you see that one?'

'No.'

He looked appalled. 'Oh, my dear . . .'

He poured himself another punch and winked at me over the top of the glass. 'Perhaps we could sit together . . .'

'Eh?'

'During the film!' he said, really getting worried about me now. 'Francis is getting the projector out now. We'd better go in the other room.'

He made a move towards the lounge and that precise moment I knew I was going to pass out. The room started to spin, slowly at first, just a gentle rocking backwards and forwards, but then it started to pick up momentum and the ceiling began to change places with the floor. Round and round, up and down and in and out—all at the same time.

I made a dive for the lounge door and ignored the protests as I belted my way through to the hall. It was like passing through Dante's incense factory. Smoke and perfume hung thick from the ceiling and a thousand mad, ugly faces rushed before my eyes like a tapestry in Hell.

I fell into the hall which was deserted and found the stairs. Then I vaguely remember crawling up them with my face pressed close to the carpet and the smell of dust rising into my nostrils. On hands and knees I stretched for a door knob and fell into a bedroom.

'Oh, shut up, will you!' said a prissy voice. 'Honest to God, there's no peace for the wicked!'

'Yes, go on out,' said his bedmate.

I fell out on to the landing again and this time found the door to the little boxroom at the back of the house. I pushed into its cool, deserted darkness and turned the key in the lock. Vaguely, by the light from the houses at the rear, I saw the divan bed tucked against the wall and I fell upon it with a sense of the greatest relief.

I suppose I must have passed out and yet not totally, because sounds drifted into my ears from time to time that caused me some concern. Shouting and banging and shrieks and curses— all intermingled and indefinite and yet sufficiently meaningful to penetrate the anaesthesia that was paralysing my whole body.

I shrugged and turned over and found a cool oasis on the mattress which blew at my sweating head and whispered, 'Nightie-night, Russell,' and I was gone.

I was doing a dem in Istanbul for the Shah of Popitinya who had just invited me to spend a fortnight in his harem when the crash against the door brought me skittering back to bewilderment.

'Anyone in there!' demanded a brute of a voice. 'Come on, we know you're in there! I'll give you five to unlock this door!'

My heart was thumping around all over my body and I

hadn't the slightest idea where I was.

'What's the matter?' I called.

'What's the matter?' answered the voice, taking the mickey. 'George, there's one in 'ere that wants to know what's the matter!'

I didn't catch George's reply but from the way my bloke laughed it must have been wildly obscene.

'Come on out, sweetie,' he said insultingly. 'We're the police!'

Something came out of the darkness and slammed me between the eyes, knocking me dizzy. Police? No ... someone was playing games. It was a practical joke and they'd discovered I'd passed out and I was the joke for tonight.

'Go away, I'm tired,' I called.

There was a moment's appalled silence and then his voice was assailing my sensibilities like the striking of a seventy-foot gong from a yard away.

'TIRED! OPEN THIS MUCKING DOOR BEFORE I BUST IT DOWN AND YOU WITH IT, YOU BLEEDIN' GREAT FAIRY. WE'RE THE POLICE!!'

You know, I really began to believe it was the police. I shot off the bed and fumbled with the door. Standing there, looking at me like I was a chunk of over-ripe Camembert that someone had stuck inside his boot, was six feet six of uniformed malevolence hell-bent on hating me to death.

'Come on, ducky....' His voice was quiet, controlled loathing. 'Come and join your girl-friends in the monkey waggon.'

From downstairs there was a babble of effeminate protests and frothy remonstrations intermingled with very masculine expostulations and physical urgings towards the front door.

I looked at my bloke and winced as his fiery black eyes cut right into me.

'Get goin',' he said quietly, his voice rumbling up from his stomach.

Oh, boy, did this need sorting out!

'Look ... there's been a mistake ...!' I said.

'There certainly has, sonny—and your father made it.'

That hurt. I could feel my temper beginning to get the better of me. 'Now, look, I'm not one of them ...!' I shouted.

He gave me a bored look. 'No, of course not. Now get downstairs, son ...'

I wasn't having any of this. 'Will you listen, officer, for just a minute ...!'

'Are you going to walk down or are you going down the hard way...'

'I'm a salesman,' I shouted. 'I came here to sell these fellows a sewing machine...'

'Tell it to the sergeant!' he shouted back, louder than I could. 'Now get!'

He got hold of my arm with a fist the size of a young pig and shoved me towards the top of the stairs. I stumbled against the banisters and shot down the stairs four at a time. When I reached the hall I couldn't believe my eyes. The place was a shambles. All the plants and the pictures had been torn off the walls and were lying in a sad, broken heap all over the floor. Then I looked into the lounge and gasped.

It looked like a Panzer division had stormed through it with orders to reduce everything to the smallest possible fragments. The beautiful white carpet was ripped and gashed and badly stained with a lot of blood and the blue three-piece suite was now a black and blue forty-seven piece suite and the kapok from the cushions was strewn around the place like multi-coloured snow.

The only intact pieces in the entire room were an 8-mm. projector which was lying on its side in the fireplace—and a sewing machine.

Sitting on the floor in one corner was a leather-jacketed bloke who had his head buried in his hands; and across the room, sitting on the floor among the debris of the shattered dining table, tears rolling silently down his bloodied face, was Francis.

Standing in the corner of the room, watching me with great interest, was the sergeant.

'Come in, son,' he said quietly. 'And where did you crawl from?'

Leather Jacket looked up briefly and then dismissed me in favour of his aching head, but Francis looked up astonished. He'd obviously forgotten all about me.

I walked into the room slowly, hearing the constable's boots thumping down the stairs behind me.

'Found 'im doin' a solo in the back bedroom, sarg. Says he's a "salesman".' I'd never heard any word said with greater implications of filth.

'Hmm,' said the sergeant. 'What d'you sell, son? Dirty films?'

His hands had been behind his back all this time but now he

brought them out front and waved a 400-feet reel of film at me.

'Lash McTaggart Meets The Chief Whip,' he said. 'One of yours? Where did you get it from?'

'I sell sewing machines,' I said.

He looked casually at the Major which was itself intact but which was hanging out of its carrying case at a crazy angle.

'You sell this?' he said, nodding at it.

I glanced at Francis. 'Yes.'

'Who to?'

I nodded at Francis. 'To him.'

'When?'

'This afternoon.'

He thought it over for a bit.

'What's your name, son?'

'Russell Tobin.'

'Address?'

I told him and I heard the constable scribbling behind me.

'Who do you sell for?'

'Ritebuy Sewing Machines.'

'Address?'

I told him that too.

'How long does it take you to sell a sewing machine—normally?'

I shrugged. My head was still spinning and the whole mess was like a bad dream. I just couldn't believe it was happening . . .

'Don't you know?' he said sarcastically.

'An hour—perhaps an hour and a half.'

'What time did you get here?'

I had to think very hard about that one. I wasn't even sure what day it was.

'About five o'clock.'

Very slowly and dramatically he brought his arm up and peeled back his sleeve to look at his watch.

'It is now . . . three and a half minutes to midnight precisely. That means you have been here almost . . . seven hours?' He looked up from his watch with exaggerated and contrived innocence. 'Tough sale?'

At that point Francis could take his sarcasm no longer.

'Oh, for heaven's sake, sergeant, leave him alone! Russell came here to sell us a machine . . .'

'Russell!' said the sergeant. 'Oh, I see . . . !'

Francis was getting his little rag out, bless him. 'No, you don't see, sergeant...!'

'Listen, you! Shut up,' roared the sergeant. 'You're in enough trouble—so don't add to it!'

I thought Francis was going to cry and I felt very sorry for him.

'Now ... Russell,' the sergeant said snidely. 'Tell us about this seven hour marathon of yours.'

I sighed and tried to look resentful.

'I started selling the machine and they gave me a glass of punch to try. I thought it was harmless stuff and I had two or three more while I was doing the dem and that's about all I can tell you.' I laughed, something just coming into my mind. 'I don't even know if they bought it.'

Francis looked up, almost hurt.

'Well, of course we bought it, duc ... er ... Russell. You've got our cheque for it.'

I looked blankly at him. 'Have I?'

Francis laughed, despite his injuries and his terrible predicament. 'My God, that punch must have been better than I thought!'

The sergeant sneered at him and said to me, 'Have you got it?'

I shrugged and went for my wallet. The cheque was there, signed by Francis, and I reckon that little bit of paper saved my life that night. The sergeant held out his hand for it so I gave it to him. He looked at it for a second and then handed it back, and when he spoke I thought I could detect a slightly more respectful tone in his voice, as though he was just beginning to believe me.

'So you're trying to tell me you had no part in what happened here tonight,' he said, stretching and sniffing.

I shrugged. 'I don't even know what *did* happen here tonight.'

He peered right into the back of my skull with narrowed eyes. 'Are you telling me you didn't know about this film?'

I sighed again and was a fraction late in answering.

'Oh, so you did know about the film!' he said, pouncing.

I suddenly felt absolutely drained, worn out. I just wanted to get out of that hell-hole and back to my own clean bed—or Samantha's—or Gloria's—or ... anyway, somewhere nice and sane and normal.

'Look, sergeant ... I did hear something. I remember stand-

157

ing by the punch-bowl in the kitchen and some weirdie in a puce sweater and maroon slacks was talking about some film but I hadn't the faintest what he was going on about. I think I must've passed out just then. I don't even remember getting upstairs.'

There was absolute silence in the room for about ten years and all the time the sergeant just stared at me with his eyes narrowed as if I was too bright for him and his cheeks sucking in and out like an anaesthetist's bladder.

When he finally spoke it almost hurt.

'You'd better watch it, son. Make sure you know what you're drinking before you swallow it next time ...' his eyes moved lethargically to Francis and when they came back to me there was a hint of a dirty smile in them, '... otherwise ... you might wake up pregnant. Right, you can go home.'

I turned towards the door and then remembered. I turned again and looked around the room.

'What is it now?' asked the sergeant.

'I had a briefcase.'

We found it stuffed up the chimney.

I looked at Francis but he was staring vacantly at his canvas casuals so I left it. I glanced at Leather Jacket but he was also full of his own troubles so I went out quickly into the hallway, stepping over the rubble all the way to the front door. The constable saw me off the premises.

'Officer ... what happened in there?' I said.

For a moment or two I thought he wasn't going to answer me but then he said gruffly, 'About eight young ruffians gatecrashed the ... er ... party and roughed the nancy boys up. Three are in hospital.'

'The fellow in the leather jacket...?'

He nodded. 'He's one of them. There was no more room in the van for those two in there.'

'Goodnight, officer.'

'Goodnight, son—and just watch it, eh?'

I half expected to see the car ripped to pieces but it wasn't. One of the windshield wipers had been bent out straight and one of the hubcaps was lying in the gutter but that, miraculously, was all.

I got home about one and fell into bed absolutely shattered. It felt so good—lying there in my own bed, in my own room. Tiny it was and it had a lousy view but that night it was a penthouse in Park Lane. It was safe and clean and cosy and I

was suddenly overwhelmed, lying there in the dark, by a yearning to go back home to the country, to smell fresh hay again and talk with the dozy old locals who were such a far cry from the nasties I'd been with that night.

But in the morning I was feeling much better.

FOURTEEN

You know, it always amazes me how much trouble you can get into just minding your own business and going about the job of living your little life—like that Francis and Peter thing, for instance.

You get out of bed in the morning feeling that life really isn't too bad after all and with one or two unexpected bonuses —like being able to get a seat on the bus or a nod of recognition from the chairman of the board in the corridor—it can be pretty marvellous, and then, right out of the blue—trouble.

You get a letter before breakfast from the Post Office threatening to cut off your phone unless you pay up and this ruins your boiled egg and toast soldiers because you know damned well you've paid it, or you pick up a woman's dropped handbag in the bus queue and she screams blue murder that you were trying to pinch it. You know what I mean, I'm sure.

Misunderstanding, that's what it is; lack of communication between two people. And I seemed to run into a whole spate of this with Tom O'Neill, our sales manager, as soon as the season of goodwill to all men was safely behind us, stowed away with relief and the decorations for another twelve months.

It had been a marvellous Christmas, it really had.

Allen Draper had told us that purse-strings would be looser and hearts more generous than ever before, and, by gum, they were, too. I had a fabulous couple of weeks just before Christmas and I started off the festive season with a great wadge of commission as thick as my Aunt Nellie's ankles—and we spent every penny of it.

When I say 'we' I mean the girls and me, of course, because I decided, after the Peter and Francis fiasco, that if I was going to get into trouble behaving myself, I might as well get into it doing the other.

It was sad about Chris and Helen, though, poor kids. Both their husbands flew home for Christmas and they couldn't join in the fun. Helen cried a bit on the phone.

But Samantha and Millie and Gloria all had a fair slice of

what was going—the money, I mean.

I spent all day Sunday—that was Christmas Eve—with Samantha at her place. Her folks had gone over to Manchester for the day to take presents to some relatives, so I rolled up about eleven in the morning with four bottles of champagne and I didn't roll out again until seven at night. What a day! It wasn't only the corks that popped, I'll tell you.

Samantha seemed determined to break some kind of world record, I think. She was incredible.

It all started when she decided to dance the Limbo and put a curtain rod across two of the empty champagne bottles on the floor in the lounge. Well, she had several tries at getting under the rod and then decided her dress was too tight, so she took it off. Then it was her stockings that were too restricting...

Anyway, she never made it under the rod, what with one thing and another, even with me helping her, but the whole idea of the dance seemed to spark off one or two other innocent indoor sports which themselves seemed a deliberate challenge to the imagination and things sort of picked up from there. It was a lovely day.

I slept a bit late on Christmas morning, not unnaturally, and Gloria's telephone call had me down in Auntie Barnes' hallway at ten o'clock in my dressing gown.

Gloria was a bit suspicious about my general state of vim and vigour even over the phone so I had a cold swill after she rang off and gave myself a good talking to and by the time I drove over to her place I was feeling quite my old perky self. Pernicious stuff, champagne. I'll never drink it again. Leaves you feeling like a dried-out chammy leather.

Christmas Day was quite a day, too. I took Gloria down to the Pier Head first of all and we had a good fast walk along the top to blow the cobwebs away. There was a fair old wind blowing up from the sea but a watery sun popped out for a bit and it didn't seem so cold after that.

She looked a treat, Gloria. She was all snuggled up in a lovely bright red coat with a white fur collar on it and I could see quite a few fellows giving her the eye as we walked along. Dirty devils.

Anyway, after we'd got some roses in our cheeks I sprang my Christmas surprise on her. I'd already told her not to cook lunch at the flat because I was taking her out to a restaurant as a little treat, but what I hadn't told her was which restaurant I had in mind.

We got in the car after our walk and drove back through town towards Brownlow Hill as if we were heading out of town, but then, at the last minute, I turned into a car park by the Adelphi Hotel.

Gloria looked around and then at me and I could see she was puzzled.

'Thought you might like a drink before lunch,' I said, not giving anything away.

'I'd love one. Where?'

'In there,' I said, nodding at the Adelphi, which, in case you don't know, is a very splendid hotel indeed.

Gloria's eyes popped. 'Oh, Russ, really? I'd love it! I've never been in there.'

So in we went.

It's funny, isn't it, how you react to the place you're in. I can walk into any old transport caff and in a couple of ticks I actually feel like one of the lads. I'm a lorry driver doing the long haul from London to Glasgow and I want a big, thick mug of hot, sweet tea in one hand and a doorstep sandwich in the other. And I wouldn't have it any other way.

But put me, on the other hand, in a place like the Adelphi cocktail bar and you're looking at the smoothest lounge-lizard that ever was. I become dapper, self-assured, accustomed to the luxury as though it was my birthright. It's all a big cod, really, because I don't know a Singapore Sling from a pint of anti-freeze, but I must say I cover my abysmal ignorance with a great deal of je ne sais quoi, as the Italians say.

Anyway, Gloria's pretty little face didn't stop shining with delight at the plush surroundings until the waiter came over to us and offered us a couple of menus about a yard and a half long and six feet wide. Then, when she realized we were eating there, her delight became flamboyant ecstasy and I thought for one heady moment she was going to leap over the table and rape me.

We had a super lunch, to say the least, and it was obvious I couldn't have pleased her more if I'd bought her a mink-trimmed Daimler. All of which was very gratifying because, being the supreme egoists we are, we do like to think our little efforts are appreciated, don't we? And it was even more gratifying for me than for most, perhaps, because Gloria couldn't stop thanking me all afternoon. She really is the most appreciative soul.

On Boxing Day evening I popped around to see Millie who

had just got back from her mum's in Preston. I'd brought her a couple of L.P.s of Tschaikovsky ballet music which pleased her no end and I was about to suggest we go upstairs and play them when old Mrs Leyevski (her landlady, you may remember) invited us into her place for a bit of cold supper. We had a fine old time for a couple of hours with her son and a few of her Jewish friends. The old girl surprised me by producing a couple of bottles of Scotch which she'd bought especially for Christmas, and although she didn't drink herself she kept us well topped-up all evening. By the time the folks started to leave Millie and I were doing quite nicely.

It was a bit awkward for me, then, because I didn't know whether to say goodnight to Millie there or what. I thought it'd look a bit blatant if I suddenly whipped her upstairs to her room in front of the old girl. But Mrs Leyevski came to the rescue, bless her. She peered at the records that Millie was carrying and said, 'Oh, Tschaikovsky, how lovely, Millie. What a lovely gift. Do you like Tschaikovsky, Mr Tobin?'

'Yes, very much,' I said.

The old girl smiled and nodded to herself, enjoying her little joke.

'Yes, I'm sure you do,' she said. 'But don't play him too loud, there's good children, because I'm going to bed. Goodnight, Mr Tobin.'

She wandered off into her front room and closed the door tightly.

Millie wiggled her nose at me, reached for my hand, and up we went to the Nutcracker Suite.

So, it was a pretty fair old Christmas, I think you'll agree, and I only hope you had one half as good. But, with the festivities over and the New Year hangovers behind us, things got very quickly back to normal. No, beg your pardon, not back to normal. Things had been going so magnificently at Ritebuy for a whole month before Christmas that we'd all begun to think of that state of affairs as being normal, but in the New Year things were anything but magnificent.

Well, it stood to reason, didn't it? Sewing machines are ideal Christmas presents and money was plentiful—ergo, we sold a bundle. But in January everybody's flatter than a slice of Spam and the last thing on earth they want to buy or can afford is a fifty quid sewing machine—ergo, disaster.

Of course, everyone at Ritebuy expected this to happen but

somehow even expecting it didn't seem to make much difference. There was an air of gloom and tension about the place that got worse and worse as the days went by. All the lads just mooched around, waiting for the leads to come in. They sat in the dem room mostly, playing cards, smoking themselves into a stupor and worrying about their H.P. payments. Tempers got a bit frayed, too—naturally, and it was during the second week of the New Year, under these conditions, that I had my first real brush with O'Neill.

I suppose, to be fair about it, O'Neill was under just as much strain as any of us, although we couldn't see it. After all, he was on salary, being in the shop, and he didn't have the money worries that the lads had. But then, he must have been under some pressure from the two partners to make certain that the absolute most was made of the few leads that were coming in.

Anyway, on the Thursday of that second week two leads came in the morning post and the only fair way to distribute them was to pop them into a hat and draw for them. Well, Johnny Brady drew one and I drew the other and while O'Neill led us out of the dem room, the other lads were settling back into the vapours quite nicely, muttering and cursing and smoking and worrying.

The way O'Neill started talking to us when we got outside would have been hilarious if the situation hadn't been so serious. He was like one of those terribly British company commanders you see in very bad films, briefing his 'chaps' before they go over the top.

'Now listen, lads,' he said, his voice low and quiet and terribly earnest. 'I think you know how much it means to Ritebuy—and to yourselves, of course—that you make these two sales today. This is a bad time of the year and every lead must count—*must* count. Now, Jimmy and Allen are doing their bit. They're spending a lot of money on advertising to give you fellows a fair deal and we mustn't let them down, must we?'

'No,' we chorused, shaking our heads.

'Go out there, lads, and sell, sell like you've never sold before. Don't take "no" for an answer. Push, push, push all the way, and if you feel like giving up, just think of the other men in there, your mates, who won't be getting a lead today and might not get another lead for a week . . .'

164

I looked up from the floor to Johnny Brady's face at this moment and disaster overtook us. Johnny has one of the funniest faces I've ever seen—even when he's being solemn. I can't describe what exactly is so funny about it but it has something to do with the colour of his eyes and the position of his eyebrows which sprout out of his head like a couple of moth-eaten paste brushes. And now, as I looked at him, he glanced at O'Neill, crossed his eyes until the pupils disappeared and yawned in utter boredom.

I just couldn't control the laughter that exploded out of me and stopped O'Neill, mouth open in disbelief, in mid-sentence.

I quickly stifled the laugh and looked suitably repentant but O'Neill was not to be appeased. His mouth worked noiselessly once or twice while his bright beady eyes bore right into me.

'Kindly tell me, Mr Tobin,' he said, breathing hard, 'what exactly I said that was so humorous.'

'I'm sorry,' I muttered. 'It wasn't anything you said . . .'

'I sincerely hope not, laddie,' he said, hurt and angry. A bright crimson flush began colouring his thin face and his eyes seemed to blaze more brightly against the darkening skin. For a minute I thought he was going to pop me one and I got myself ready to pop him right back.

At last he stopped glaring at me and transferred his venom to Johnny who by now was looking so demurely innocent that I damn-near burst out laughing again.

After giving Johnny an adequate dose of hate, O'Neill turned away, saying, 'I'll see you both when you come back. I hope, for your sakes, that you're successful.'

And there was more than a hint of threat in that little lot, I can tell you.

Out in the yard, Johnny said, 'Silly little bastard, who does he think he is, talking to us like that? He'll have to watch himself, will Mr O'Neill, or he'll find himself with a mouthful of Ritebuy Minor.'

'There's plenty of room for a Major,' I said. 'And a couple of trade-ins.'

Well, as I said, you never know where trouble is coming from and at what time of the day or night. If you did, I suppose you'd shoot yourself as soon as you were old enough to hold a gun, so it's just as well. My little lot came about half an hour after leaving the yard, in the depths of the country, way out beyond Childwall.

Even in these days of intense building you still don't have to go too far out of the big cities to find countryside, and just on the outskirts of Liverpool there's plenty of it. My lead was to a Mrs Gladys Furnborough in a little place called Ashfield and I was very much looking forward to the run out.

Having been stuck in the morbid atmosphere of Ritebuy for most of the week the prospect of getting not only out of the shop but out of the city was a most attractive one and I was bowling along very nicely, doing a steady forty and looking around at the bleak countryside, waving at the cows and talking to the pigs, when suddenly it happened. With a hiss and a whoosh my radiator blew up and a spray of dark brown antifreeze shot all over the windshield. At first I thought I'd run through a muddy puddle but then it began to dawn even on my unmechanical mind that things were very much amiss.

I drove the car on to a narrow scrap of grass verge and got out. Steam was blowing in great hissing gusts from under the bonnet, so I let things cool off a bit before inspecting the damage. Gingerly I lifted the bonnet and peered inside as if I knew what I was looking for. All I could see was a very wet engine.

I looked up the road and down the road and all around me. There wasn't a house or a car or a farm or a human being in sight. There wasn't even a cow or a pig. I might well have been standing in the middle of the Yukon.

Well, now, I'm not going to impose my tale of woe upon you. I will not tell you how I waited on that perishing country road, sitting in the car, getting out again, jumping up and down and swinging my arms like an idiot to prevent frostbite and gangrene setting in, for over an hour before I got a car to stop and take me into the village.

I will not labour you with the frustration I suffered trying to get that yokel garage to tow me in for repairs, their one and only tow-truck being unavailable until after lunch because it was busy pulling some poor basket out of two feet of mud on a farm road.

I refuse on principle to burden you by relating how the garage had spares for just about every car under the sun (including a headlamp for a Bull-nose Morris) except for a particular type of Hillman, of which mine was one, and of how the spare parts had to be sent for to the nearest Hillman dealer who, by the time it took, must have been situated sixteen miles north of Edinburgh.

Nothing would induce me to tell of the number of attempts I

made to telephone Mrs Furnborough to warn her of my difficulties and that on each occasion I failed to get through, owing, largely, to the fact that no one answered the phone.

I will, however, just mention that when I finally completed the journey from the garage to her home, having parted with enough of my money for a fortnight's holiday in the Wankie Game Reserve, I discovered a little pencilled note on her front door which read, 'Please see next door'.

I saw next door and the grey-haired old darling behind it told me ever so nicely that Mrs Furnborough had gone to Shropshire for three days and did apologize for sending in the coupon so hastily. Could I call back in February, she said.

O'Neill was waiting for me when I finally got back, cold and utterly miserable, that evening. He was in a foul mood.

'Well, now, welcome back, Mr Tobin. This must surely be an all-time record for one call. Where in hell have you been, lad?'

I think it was at this moment that I realized I'd had enough of sewing machines and Ritebuy and Tom O'Neill and the whole flaming issue, although I didn't actually quit until some weeks later.

FIFTEEN

Well, you can't go on taking it for ever, can you?

As I mentioned quite a while back, if you find yourself in a position where life is becoming unbearable through some megalomaniacal jackass coming the old aggie all the time then you really have no choice—if you want to stay sane, that is. You either run the sod over on a dark night or you leave.

O'Neill got no better after that little do. I took a lot from him that evening but I was too tired to argue with him. I just stayed chup and let him rant and rave for a bit and then I quietly told him what had happened and walked out, leaving him muttering to himself.

I thought, in my innocence, that there might be some sort of apology from him the next morning, but it was not forthcoming. On the contrary, he seemed to get worse, as if by keeping quiet I'd shown him up as being the bad-tempered basket he was.

Nothing serious happened afterwards, mind you, but there were lots of little things—sly digs in front of the other lads about cleanliness (the time I stepped into a puddle in the yard and walked into the shop with dirty shoes) or about carelessness (when I left my briefcase behind in a customer's house over a week-end). You know the sort of things. In themselves they weren't too important but added together they began to point to Tom O'Neill and yours truly fast becoming very firm enemies.

Well, February blew itself into March and things got no better between us. Then, one morning, I was late—through no fault of my own—and O'Neill bollocked me good and proper in front of the other lads. Well, I flipped. I was jumping up and down with resentment and we started a good old-fashioned slanging match which had Allen Draper scuttling out of his office and desperately trying to smooth things over.

But the writing was on the proverbial wall after that. One more crack from that little twit and he would get it—even if it meant me getting mine.

And two days later it happened.

It was Friday, as luck would have it, because these things always work out better if they happen at the end of the week. It's tidier, isn't it? If it's nothing too serious then you've got the week-end to quieten down and get things in perspective, and if it is serious, then you've got the week-end to look for another job. A good day for battle is Friday.

Anyway, the last call of that day was to a Mrs Soul—and a very old soul was she, living all alone, bless her, in a frightful room at the top of a big old house.

She welcomed me in as though I was the first human being she'd seen for months (which I might well have been) and bustled around making me a cup of tea and breaking open a new packet of biscuits. She chattered away cheerfully all the time she was doing this, though what she had to be cheerful about completely escaped me.

What a depressing place. It was chilly, dark and smelled of damp and the only source of comfort in the room was a decrepit gas fire which, going full blast, gave out about as much warmth as a red-hot knitting needle.

Well, we chatted for a bit and then I showed her the Minor, although the room was so dark it's a wonder she could see me, never mind the machine, and when I'd finished she said she'd have it.

She took out a battered black leather purse from her pinny— it was a plain black one, I remember—just like my gran used to wear—and she had a lot of trouble getting the five one-pound notes out because her fingers were a bit stiff—either from rheumatics or the cold or maybe a bit of both.

I took the money and made her receipt out and then, of course, it was time for me to leap downstairs and bring up the Major. But in my entire time at Ritebuy I had never been so certain I was wasting my time and energy as I was at that moment. I knew I couldn't sell a Major to this old darling in a fortnight of Passion Sundays. Well, it was sticking out like Southend pier, wasn't it?

Firstly, she would obviously never be able to afford the payments out of her scrap of pension. Secondly, she'd never have any use for a lolloping great machine like the Major, even if she could lift the thing on to the table, which she couldn't. And, thirdly, she was so old that an H.P. company would never have signed her up for even a three-day contract without worrying a bit.

But, nevertheless, I felt I had to go through the motions, so I

169

nipped downstairs, lugged up the Major and half-heartedly started the spiel.

As I expected, when I got to the close and told her she could have the machine for a fiver down and pay the balance off over three years, she fell about laughing.

'Young man,' she cackled, 'I'll be very happy and very lucky if I live for another three months, never mind three years. No, dearie, thank you for showing it to me, but this little one will do nicely for the bit of sewing I've got to do.'

And, of course, I agreed with her. And what was more, I knew right then that I was going no further with the spiel. I was not going to kill the sale on the Minor; I was not going to tell her she'd have to wait three weeks for a machine; I was not going to try to flog her some beaten-up trade-in with a cheap motor stuck on it. If this old darling wanted the Minor, she could have it. So she got it.

You know, I walked downstairs to the car feeling wonderful. I felt light, carefree—free, somehow, even though I had a pretty good idea I'd just committed professional suicide as far as Ritebuy was concerned—or maybe it was because I knew it. I must have been balmy because I was actually looking forward to seeing O'Neill's face when I told him.

He was waiting for me when I got back to the shop, although he was trying to make out he wasn't. He was fiddling with a cabinet model when I walked in and he continued to fiddle with it for a bit before finally sauntering across towards me. I could sense the tension and dislike behind his painfully casual manner.

'Well,' he said, 'how d'you make out today, lad?'

I took out my cigarettes and proceeded to light one.

'A Major and a Minor,' I said, being as casual as he was.

It took a moment for it to sink in, then, slowly, the frown crept down from his hair-line and the disbelief clouded his eyes.

'A Minor!' he said, as if I'd just told him there were eight dead salesmen in the yard.

'Yes,' I said, still casual, although my heart was leaping around all over the place now. The fight was on, I could smell it coming, and I welcomed it. Come on, come and get me, little man. I want to be got. Round one, seconds out. No mercy. Each man for himself.

'What d'you mean, you "sold" a Minor?' he said, his voice hard and quivery. 'You mean you couldn't kill the sale, don't

170

you, Tobin? You didn't deliberately leave a Minor, did you?'

I let him stew a little while I took a long drag on my cigarette and wiped some smoke out of my eye.

'Tobin, I asked you a question!' he said and his anger sounded unmistakably at my impertinence.

I looked around the shop. Two of the lads were in one of the demonstration booths and were obviously listening to all this while pretending not to.

I turned again to O'Neill who by now was becoming nicely puce.

'Shall we go in the dem room?' I said. 'I don't want to talk here.'

After a quiet fume he strode off across the shop and burst into the dem room. I followed with deliberate leisure and closed the door behind me with aggravating care. I turned to face him.

'In answer to your question—yes, I deliberately sold and left a Minor.'

I wondered, with surprisingly detached interest, whether this was going to develop into a punch-up. The way he was standing there with his mouth working like a beached porpoise gave me the idea that he might just do something nasty and I found myself trying to decide where I'd hit him if he did.

I've never been what you'd call a 'physical' fellow, although I had my normal quota of ding-dongs at school, and the thought intrigued me. And although I'd usually take a very big detour to avoid a scrap, I knew I could make a happy exception with this little squirt, especially if it meant easing someone else's burden in the future.

I decided I'd kick him in the stomach.

'You *deliberately* sold a *Minor*, lad?'

I sighed wearily. 'Mr O'Neill, while we're on the subject, please don't ever call me "lad" again. You have no idea how it irks me.'

I thought his face was going to burst. It was now swollen to enormous proportions like an over-inflated purple balloon and he looked so pompous and preposterous that I couldn't resist saying, 'You ought to see a doctor. I think you're constipated.'

'Oooohhh!' he went, letting go all the pent-up breath in one mighty whoosh. 'How *dare* you!'

'And how dare you!' I shouted. 'There's only one God, you know, and he's up there . . .'

He took a step towards me, threatening in the extreme, and

I drew my foot back, eyeing his nether regions as though I was taking aim. He stopped dead, shocked, sobered that I could do such a thing.

'You're FIRED, Tobin!' he shouted. 'You're fired, LAD!'

I couldn't help smiling, he looked so pathetic. I shook my head, 'No, little man, I quit.'

He threw himself at the door and stamped down the corridor to Jimmy Sands' office, and by the time I reached the corridor Sands, Draper and O'Neill were rushing out.

'Mr Tobin,' Sands called. 'Russ—just a minute!'

O'Neill was scowling in the background, still breathing hard and dying to tear my arms off, and Allen Draper was just looking his nice old bewildered self.

'Russ,' said Sands, coming up to me. 'What's all the trouble?'

I shrugged. 'No trouble, Jimmy. Mr O'Neill and I just don't see eye to eye, that's all.'

Sands frowned and looked very perturbed. 'Oh, now, I'm sure...'

I shook my head and stopped him with my hand. 'No, Jimmy. I've been through all this before. I don't even want to discuss it.' I looked very directly at O'Neill. 'I can't stand the sight of him and he can't stand the sight of me. One of us would have to leave and I choose to.'

Sands spun round, perplexed, to look at O'Neill and then turned back to me.

'But ... have you got something to go to? Have you got another job lined up?'

'No,' I said. 'But I'll find something.'

I put my hand out to him. 'Thank you, Jimmy.'

He put his out, uncertainly, but shook mine nevertheless.

'I've got some machines in the car,' I said. 'I'll take them in to Charlie.'

Old Charlie was just about to pack up for the night when I lugged the two Majors in and plonked them down in the stockroom. He stopped what he was doing and looked irritably at the machines and then at me.

'What's wrong with them, then? They were sewing perfec'ly when they left here.'

I grinned at him. 'They're still perfect, Charlie. I'm turning them in. I'm leaving.'

'Oh,' he said, quite unsurprised. 'Moving on?'

I shrugged. 'Somewhere.'

This raised his ancient eyebrows half a millimetre but he still continued to wipe the oil from his hands with a bit of rag.

'Nothing definite, then?'

'No, not yet.'

And then he was smiling slyly and chortling quietly to himself, as if a familiar pattern of human behaviour was once again presenting itself to him and he was delighted that some things, at least, never changed in an otherwise confusing and ever-changing world.

'Itchy feet?' he asked, cocking an amused eye at me.

'Yes, Charlie. Also I can't stand O'Neill.'

He scowled at the name and 'humph-ed'.

'Me, neither, but he's got the sense to keep out of my way. He tried to come the madam with me when he first came here and I warned him to stay out or I'd stick him with me screwdriver. He's hardly been in since.'

He finished wiping his hands and stowed the rag away behind the bench.

'But it's not only him, though, is it,' he said, placing some tools carefully in the rack. 'I don't think he could scare you away if you really wanted to stay. I think you were about to leave anyway.'

He's a shrewd old bloke, Charlie. He knows what you're thinking almost before you do. If ever a man was wasted in a job like this. He should have been doing an E.S.P. act round the halls.

'No, Charlie, it's not just him. I'm getting a bit fed up with these things.'

I kicked at a Major on the floor.

'Come to think of it, I'm bloody sick of them.'

He turned to me, laughing, and held out his hand.

'You'd never be half as sick of them as I am, Russ, but I'm stuck with them now. I'm glad you're not. Good luck, lad. All the best.'

'Thanks for everything, Charlie.'

'You're welcome. Take care, now.'

As I reached the door, he said, surprisingly, 'Dissatisfaction has always been misunderstood, Russ—but only by the cosy-minded. You go on being dissatisfied until you find what's right for you, lad. It's a blinkin' short life.'

'Thanks, Charlie. I'll remember that.'

I went out into the yard and got in the car, and for a

moment or two I sat there, looking around me at all the familiar things. Then I started thinking back over the year, recalling faces and trying to put names to them, remembering the good times and feeling the bad ones elude my memory. And so blinkin' what, I thought.

I started the engine and drove out of the yard for the last time.

It's a funny old life, isn't it? Round and round the garden, like a teddy bear. One step, two steps—stick your roots down —where?

Thing is to keep cheerful, isn't it? Something always seems to turn up, somehow. Don't you find that?

I'll never regret leaving Ritebuy. I've got a marvellous job now, really marvellous.

I work for an American finance house—Karefree Kredit Inkorporated—and I'm employed under the exalted title of Supernumerary Finance Account Control Supervisor. Sounds terrific, doesn't it?

Actually, a debt collector is what I am, and very interesting it can be at times, too, as you might imagine.

Anyway, I won't bore you with that now. Maybe some other time. But you wouldn't believe the things people do rather than pay their debts, you really wouldn't.

Only the other day this gorgeous little custard, who was up to her pretty eyeballs in trouble, invited me in and asked me whether there wasn't some sort of personal arrangement we could come to . . .